Dream Hitcher

Books by F.M. Parker

Coldiron *series*
Coldiron
Shadow of the Wolf
The Shanghaiers
Thunder of Cannon
Spoils of War (a.k.a. The Thieves)

Novels
Dream Hitcher (a.k.a. The Hitcher)
The Highwayman
The Last Orphan Train (a.k.a. Girl in Falling Snow)
Soldiers of Conquest

Coming Soon!
The Assassins (a.k.a. A Score to Settle)

Dream Hitcher

F. M. Parker

SPEAKING VOLUMES, LLC
NAPLES, FLORIDA
2024

Dream Hitcher (a.k.a. The Hitcher)

Copyright © 2012 by F. M. Parker

All rights reserved. No part of this book may be reproduced or transmitted in any form or by any means without written permission.

ISBN 979-8-89022-205-3

"Even a dream is only a dream."
—by Calderon de la Barca

You know a dream is like a river
Ever changing as it flows
And a dreamer's just a vessel
That must follow where it goes.
from "The River"
—by Garth Brooks, Victoria Shaw

Chapter One

Two white men fought bare-knuckled in an iron cage erected in the vacant end of the warehouse on the Chicago waterfront. Bright lights glare down from overhead and upon the fighters to show their expressions, every blow thrown. The cage was octagonal in shape and thirty feet in diameter. The thin iron rods forming the walls of the cage were spaced eight inches apart and thus allowed a clear view of the fighters to the four hundred plus shouting, cursing men and women seated or standing in the tiered bleachers surrounding the cage.

This was not a fight with Marquis of Queensberry rules. The crowd had paid to see blood and they would get it for this was a brutal slugfest without a referee. The fight would continue until one man was beaten so badly that he couldn't get up from the dirty canvas and must be carried from the cage.

Stoddard had thirty pounds on Dan Gallatin and four inches of reach with his big fists. Both men are in great physical shape, their muscles rippling and cording beneath their skins. Gallatin was the younger man. He had reddish hair, the color of iron left out in the rain to rust, and pale white skin.

Stoddard wore a cocky, confident grin as he bored in on Dan. He tried to clench with his smaller opponent. Dan jabbed two blows into Stoddard's face. They did no real harm to Stoddard. Still they slowed him and allowed Dan to slide out of reach, and retreat, his expression showing half fright and great regret at having ever entered the cage.

Dan tripped and his guard dropped. Stoddard lunged in to strike. Dan back-peddled frantically, the scared expression in his eyes even more prominent. He throws a look through the bars of the cage, and over the head of the hard-faced promoter, Krakoff, sitting in the first row of the bleachers, to Dobbs moving among the fight fans taking bets with Dan's money. Dobbs was a little man and moving quickly, busy shoving money into his bulging coat pockets, hastily scribbling bets and odds on slips of paper and thrusting them into the hands of the bettors.

Dan turned back to Stoddard. The man had closed on him and now threw a jab. Dan dodged to the side and the fist only caught the corner of his mouth and burned the side of his face as it slid past. Immediately Stoddard swung his right fist. Dan stepped backward to lessen the power of the blow and threw up a blocking hand. Still the blow landed and jarred him. The man was damn strong and a lucky punch of one of his big fists could put Dan flat on the canvas and end the fight. He wiped at the trickle of blood that had started to flow from his cut lip.

Stoddard followed after Dan and forced him backward around the ring. Dan struck back, his blows timid as if he was afraid to anger the larger man.

On all side the fight fans were standing and howling curses and shaking their fists. A man in the front row shouted, "Kill him Stoddard. Finish him." A woman higher up in the stands, cried out, "Fight Gallatin, you damn coward. Stand and fight. Don't lose me my bet, you bastard."

Dan raised his fist to cover himself and shot a quick look at Dobbs. The man put the money from the last bet into a pocket and turned toward the cage. He saw Dan looking and raised a hand high to signal the betting was finished.

Dan turned back to Stoddard. The man was close upon him with fists cocked to strike. Dan coiled, tightened his fist and sprang to meet Stoddard. He drove a flurry of savage blows onto the bigger man's face. A cut opened over Stoddard's left eye and blood flowed.

Stoddard was hurt. And damned surprised. He backed away to gain some distance and some time to re-evaluate his opponent and mount a defense against the unexpected attack.

Dan followed after Stoddard, staying within reach and kept pounding him with both fists. A hard knuckled blow slipped past Stoddard's guard and flattened his nose. Blood streamed down over his mouth. Stoddard roared with anger, spitting blood. He lunged forward and clenched with Dan. They were head to head.

"I'm going to kill you, you son-of-a-bitch," Stoddard growled.

"Like hell, Stoddard. You're not man enough. Even with steroids."

"Bullshit. I'll show you."

Dan laughed wickedly. "Then let's get to it."

Dan butted Stoddard in the face, weakening his hold and instantly thrust both arms against Stoddard's chest. With muscles bulging, he pressed Stoddard away, twisted and broke free. He gave Stoddard a solid jab to the mouth and danced away. Dan really enjoying hitting Stoddard.

Stoddard followed after Dan and landed two good blows to his body. Stoddard gave Dan a "How did you like that?" look.

Dan's expression of pleasure didn't change. He tucked in his chin and sprang in before Stoddard could put up his guard. Dan pummeled Stoddard with both fists, landing smashing blows to the man's bleeding face, then lower to the body, then back again to the mangled face. It was total slaughter.

Dan struck a powerful right handed blow to Stoddard's jaw. The man dropped to his knees. Dan leaned down beside Stoddard and slammed a fist into the side of his face. Stoddard's head snapped to the side and blood sprayed. Stoddard collapsed face down upon the dirty canvas.

Dan leaned lower over Stoddard and whispered, "How do you feel now, Stoddard?"

Stoddard struggled weakly to hands and knees and spat blood and a tooth onto the canvas. "Goddamn you, Gallatin."

"If you can still talk, then you need another one." Dan propped Stoddard's bloody face up with his left hand and hammered it mightily with his right. The blow drove the man down flat and motionless upon the canvas.

Every spectator was now on his, or her, feet and roaring. Curses and cries of regret poured from the losers. Jubilation rang in the voices of the few winning bettors.

Dan straightened and stood over the fallen Stoddard. He stared out at the crowd. His expression said that he didn't give a rat's ass about the crowd, neither the losers nor the winners.

The spectators fall silent and stared back at Dan. The silence held for a handful of seconds as the people came to realize Dan had hoodwinked them with his act of fear and cowardice. The trance broke and the crowd began to file down from the bleachers.

The pissed off and grumbling losers gave Dan hard looks as they made for the exit to the street.

The handful of winners dug out their betting chits and, with big smiles, hurried toward Dobbs to collect.

Dan wiped blood from his cut lip and brushed it off on his trunks. He went out through the door of the cage and walked to Krakoff and Dobbs standing together.

Krakoff gave Dan an angry look and spoke in a sour tone. "You shouldn't have made it look so goddamned easy. Should'a made it last a few minutes longer. Hell you should'a sweated a little. That's if you want to fight with odds on your side in the future."

"Whether or not I fight again doesn't mean crap to me." Dan replied.

"Maybe so, but I've got to keep these nutty fans coming to see my fights."

Dan shrugged and held out his hand. Krakoff handed him a sheaf of bills.

"A thousand as we agreed. Real easy money."

"Well, if it's so damn easy, then you get in the ring next time and do the fighting."

Dan turned to the Dobbs. "What've you got for me?"

Dobbs dug bills from a pocket and began to count. He finished and stripped a few bills off the top. "A little over thirty-six hundred left after I took my ten percent. The odds got up to four to one there at the end. You sure fooled the suckers with that scared look. That trick was worth half of what you won."

"Thanks for handling the betting."

"Sure, any time. But you shouldn't have hit Stoddard that last time for he was down and out."

"Maybe so, but it felt damn fine doing it."

Dobbs shook his head, said nothing.

"You want another fight this coming Saturday night?" Krakoff asked. "I know a big black who I'm sure would like to try you on for size."

"Nope, maybe in a month or so," Dan replied. "When I need more money."

"Call me when you want to smash somebody and see some more blood."

Dan flashed angry and clenched his hands into fists around the packets of money. He had never liked Krakoff, a man who made his living off other men's pain and blood. Dan stiff armed Krakoff in the chest with a knuckled fist, propelling the man backward three steps before he could catch himself.

Dan followed after Krakoff and glared into his face. "Maybe I should smack you around and see some of your blood."

Krakoff hastily put up his hands with palms out. "Hold on now. I was just joking with you."

Dan controlled himself with an effort and gave the promoter a menacing look. "I don't like jokes when they're on me so you'd better keep your damn mouth shut."

He wheeled away. Grabbed his pants off a chair and stuffed the money into a pocket. Pulled the pants on over his trunks. Slid into his shirt, buttoned the bottom half and jammed it down into his pants. He snatched up a heavy coat and pulled it on as he headed off across the warehouse toward the exit.

Dan glanced back at Stoddard. The man had made it to his knees with blood leaking from his smashed face onto the canvas. Dan's expression showed only curiosity as he turned away.

He came out of the warehouse and into the November night lying black and cold upon the waterfront of Lake Michigan. A stiff wind, damp and heavy with lake water, drove in and rocked the half score of big lake steam ships moored to the long concrete piers, and hurried onward to wash over Dan and flop the tails of his coat. The rasping scrape of the iron side of the nearest ship against the pier came to Dan.

He pulled his coat tightly about him to ward off the bite of the wind and looked both ways along the quay. With a morose expression, he hunched his shoulders against the wind and moved off to the nearest pier, and along it with birthed ships all dark and silent looming against the moonless sky above him. At the end, he halted and stared out across the wave-tossed lake and listened to the wet slapping sound the waves made as they struck the pier. A distant ferry sounded a lonesome, forlorn call.

Dan nodded to himself, his face holding a glum, thoughtful expression. Dobbs was correct, he should not have struck Stoddard that last time. He must control those impulses to strike out and maim, but, OH HELL, how right they seem at the time.

He turned and walked back along the pier. The nearest subway station was far off, but that was all right for a long walk would give him time to do some needed thinking about his violent impulses to strike out in anger.

Chapter Two

In the front lobby of the big Barnes & Noble bookstore, Admiral Harold Essex, Retired, was standing behind a table and signing copies of his best seller, MY LIVES THROUGH TIME, for a line of several people. Essex wore a full dress military uniform with much gold braid and left chest full of medals. He was tall, with a touch of gray hair and very military, an imposing figure of a man. He was enjoying himself immensely.

A huge man-size sign of the book cover declared the book to be the best seller for the past six weeks. The cover showed Essex dressed in English naval uniforms of different time periods, a ship's gunnery officer in 1805, a seaman in 1644, ships captain in 1516.

This was one of B & N's big super stores with long racks of books, reading areas with plush chairs, and a coffee bar. The store was crowded with browsers, readers, and buyers. Several people were seated in comfortable chairs and listening to ESSEX talk as he signed books.

Other people were seated among the nearby book stacks close enough to hear Essex make his sales pitch. One of them was a big, strongly built man sitting mostly hidden from Essex by a rack of books. He was dressed in dark gray; trousers, shirt and jacket. The clothing was simple in design but expensive. Now and again, he turned a page of the book he held and pretended to read. His attention was focused on Essex. He called himself ANUBIS.

"I've relived portions of eleven past lives in dreams," said Essex. "They are just short snatches of time and not whole lives for that would take another lifetime for each one. Added all together the time that I have spent reliving those lives would add to several years. In every one I was a sailor, sometimes a crewman, sometimes an officer."

He gave a broad Navy smile to the pretty brunette with the gorgeous breast standing at the front of the line offering her book for signature. He liked small women with big breast and big brown eyes.

"Admiral Essex, how do you know you are actually experiencing a portion of a past life and not just dreaming?" asked Pretty Woman.

"Miss, I truly did live those lives. I'm sure because I have knowledge of things that I couldn't possibly know without having lived in those times. I know the names of ancient ships, names of crew members of those ships and the names of government officials of the seaports where my ship docked. I've gone to England and researched the old records of the ships and the cities and found that what I have relived was correct."

"How far back can your remember your other lives?"

"The oldest year that I recall having lived was 1516."

"Which one was the most interesting?"

Essex focused more closely on Pretty Woman and gave her a more thorough look-over. He thoughtfully rubbed his chin as he considered the question, and what he would like to do to Pretty Woman.

She showed fluster and looked down. After but a moment, she raised her head and looked directly back at Essex. She had decided his scrutiny was pleasing.

Essex liked her reaction. He spoke, "Each life was damn . . . darn interesting. But I suppose the one that was most memorable was the one where I was a young gunnery officer on Admiral Horatio Nelson's flagships HMS Victory. That was in the battle at Trafalgar in the Atlantic off Spain's western coast. That's where we British, I was a Britisher then, fought and defeated the combined fleets of Spain and France on October 21, 1805."

Essex fell silent and turned his face up at the ceiling. He seemed to be reliving that battle. After a handful of seconds, he looked back at Pretty Woman. Essex was misty eyed with the remembrance.

"Yes. It would have to be the battle at Trafalgar. We all wept when we learned that Admiral Nelson had been shot and killed."

Pretty Woman was embarrassed by Essex's sorrow. Silently she handed her book to him. He signed the fly leaf with a flourish of his pen. Closed the book and handed it to her.

"Some of my past lives weren't pleasant," Essex said to Pretty Woman. "But in all of them, I had some very beautiful women as wives and friends. I miss them very much. I hope I find a beautiful woman here in Chicago."

Pretty Woman wasn't sure how to take Essex's words. Had a pass been made at her, a proposition? She turned away pondering that question.

Essex quickly signed the books of the people, and giving each person a smile as he did so. When the last person turned away, he picked up a copy of his book, tucked it under an arm and strode toward the exit. Several people followed him out of the store and into the night washed away by bright street lights. One of the people following was Anubis.

Essex halted and motioned with his hand at the nearby parking lot. In but a half minute, a chauffeured sedan swiftly wheeled up and Essex climbed into the rear seat. The sedan sped away.

Anubis hastened toward the parking area where he hurriedly jumped into a black Porsche and sped off following the tail lights of Essex's vehicle.

Dream Hitcher

* * * * *

Admiral Essex's sedan sped along the street of large homes in the Ritzy suburbs of Chicago. The Admiral was resting his head on the back of the seat and never looked behind. He roused and sat erect when his vehicle turned into the driveway of his home and continued along it through the large trees that overhung the way.

The chauffeur stopped the car in front of the big two story house and Essex got out. Jangling keys in his hand, he walked to the front door, bearing his coat of Arms, and entered. A light came alive and shined out the windows.

The sedan rolled on to a four-car garage where the chauffeur parked it in one of the bays in the garage. The chauffeur locked the garage and hastened up a flight of stairs to the apartment over the garage. A moment later a light showed in a window.

* * * * *

Anubis slowly rolled his Porsche past the entrance of Essex's driveway and checked along its dark length. Nothing worrisome was visible and he drove on and parked on the street half a block distant. He climbed out of the vehicle, glanced both ways along the street and found it deserted. He walked unhurriedly to the driveway and vanished in among the trees bordering it.

Moving warily and silently, he made his way to the front yard of the house. There he looked for light in the windows, noting the one in the main house and the one in the garage apartment. He glanced about and saw a marble bench under the big oak tree and seated himself. Though the game was in motion, he would have to wait, and that angered him for he was not a patient man - and it had been days and far too long since the last time he had gone seeking.

Anubis sat motionless, showing nothing of the urgency gnawing at him as he watched the house. Finally the light in the garage apartment went black. Shortly thereafter the light in the downstairs of the main house blinked out and one appeared in an upstairs window.

Anubis didn't move. He sat quietly, a black statue in the night, and watched the house.

Finally the lighted window of the house went dark. Anubis made a slight nod and went back to stillness.

A handful of minutes later, Anubis rose to his feet. He carefully looked around and examined the night shadows among the trees. Finding nothing threatening, he began to pull on a pair of gloves as he stole toward the house. He moved along the side checking the windows for one unlocked. At the rear of the house, and not having found an unlocked window, he chose one and put his big hands on the frame and exerted upward pressure. And with more pressure, really leaning into the task. The latch broke and fell to the floor inside with only a little clank.

Anubis listened intently. There was no movement, no sound from inside the house. He raised the window and climbed inside.

He surveyed the room, identifying a well equipped kitchen, stove, double refrigerator, pots and pans hanging on metal hooks, table, chairs, the ordinary array of cooking equipment. He moved out into the hallway and stealthily along it to a large room, which he crossed and onward to a stairway leading upward.

He climbed noiselessly to the landing of the upper floor. There he began to quietly open the doors fronting onto the landing to peer inside. He found the room he wanted and entered. On the far side of the room near the window, Essex lay sleeping on a king-size bed.

Anubis crept up to the bed and stood looking down at the sleeper bathed in moonlight coming in through the window. The admiral's gray hair shone as silver in the moonlight. His face was turned upward as he journeyed in the Land of Nod.

Anubis leaned close to Essex and listened to his regular breathing for a few seconds. Then quietly, and ever so slowly, with the utmost care, he lay down beside Essex on the bed. He gently placed his head on the pillow but a fraction of an inch from that of Essex.

Anubis opened his mind and reached out to Essex, searching for the correct wave length, for the compatible frequency to make a connection with that of the man's thoughts. As their minds joined, Anubis heard the familiar hum of an active mind, the sound like that of a hive of bees at a distance. A kaleidoscope of colorful and swiftly shifting, indistinct pictures came quickly to flash across Anubis' inner eye. The humming sound faded rapidly. Then it ceased altogether and a picture solidified, one of a live, active scene.

Anubis saw and felt what Essex did for he had merged with the man. He was a ship's captain and standing on the quarter deck of an early 1800's warship under full sail. His face held a taut, worried expression as he stared ahead across a limitless expanse of wind tossed, blue-green ocean.

He heard the strum of the ship's taut sails and rigging and the creak of the ship's hull and splash and slide of live water along her side as she moved across the sea. He looked up at the three tall masts where every one was crammed with all possible canvas, with every sail, jib, and spanker full and pulling. The flag of a British warship flew from the peak of the main mast.

He checked the deck where twenty red-coated marines with their muskets and swords were mustered amidships. The bare-footed gun crews were at their stations. They were stripped down to their pants.

The powder monkeys, boys of twelve or thirteen, had also stripped off their jumpers and their young bodies showed bony ribs through white skins.

The captain, and Anubis, looked astern. Two large French warships plowed the waves a long cannon shot behind.

As Anubis looked, two gray plumes of gunsmoke erupted from the French ships' bow chasers. The captain raised his arm and made to call out to signal his crew of the coming missiles.

Back on the bed in the real world, Essex's arm was raised as in his dream. He brought his arm down smartly and struck Anubis hard across the chest. At the blow striking Anubis, the old seaman snapped awake and jerked to a sitting position on the bed. Anubis abruptly sat up beside him.

Essex flung a look to the side and saw Anubis. "Goddamn!" he exclaimed, his face flashing alarm. He hurled himself toward the opposite side of the bed.

Anubis caught Essex by the shoulder and yanked him back and pressed him down on the bed. He leaned on Essex and held him pinned.

Essex struggled fiercely. To no avail for Anubis with his greater strength held him captive.

"Easy, admiral," Anubis said chuckling. "You have no chance against me. You were a fine, brave warrior in your time, but I could handle you in your best days. And besides, everything is just fine."

"What the hell do you mean fine?" roared Essex. "Who are you? What do you want?"

"As to my name, call me Anubis. I'm a person who travels strange paths. And what do I want. I've come to dream one of your past lives with you. But sorrowfully now that you're awake, that's impossible."

"Go dream your own damn dreams."

"Ah. There I have a problem. I can't dream. I envy you who can dream and have access to other worlds."

"Everybody dreams when they sleep."

"You're wrong," Anubis said sadly. "When I sleep, I fall into a black pit. An endlessly deep pit where there's no light, no sound. Just a black nothingness. So you see, I must join other peoples' dreams."

Anubis paused and looked down at Essex. "I'll admit something to you Admiral. I'm addicted to dreams. Do you remember what Shakespeare wrote about dreams In The Tempest?"

"I don't give a damn what Shakespeare said about dreams."

"I shall tell you anyway. He wrote, - It is a sleep language, and thou speak'st out of thy sleep. What is it thou did'st say? This is a strange repose, to be asleep with eyes open: standing, speaking, moving, and yet is fast asleep."

"Don't quote Shakespeare to me. Get the hell out of my house and go see a doctor before I call the police."

"Oh, I'll leave. But I don't intend to leave empty handed."

"Take what you want."

"You have denied me the opening act of this evening's entertainment by awakening too soon. So now we must jump ahead to the second act and the third and final one. We'll call this night's entertainment a gift from you to me. The gift is your ultimate and grandest dream."

Essex is dumfounded. What is this crazy man telling him? "Entertainment? What the hell are you talking about?"

"You'll find out. But first, do you know who Anubis was to the ancient Egyptians?"

"What the hell has that got to do with anything?"

"Just answer the question."

Essex spoke hurriedly. "He was God of the Underworld. Or so the ancient Egyptians thought."

"He was much more than that. He weighed the hearts of the dead to decide whether or not the person had lived a good life and was worthy of everlasting life. And he had other powers. He could foresee a person's destiny and so he knew when that person would die." Anubis paused, then continued. "I foresee your destiny, admiral."

Essex has gotten the point and his face twists with fear. "You goddamn sonofabitch. You mean to kill me."

Essex suddenly exerted all his strength and tore an arm free. He struck Anubis in the face.

Anubis recaptured the arm, slammed it down on the bed and jammed a knee upon it to hold it in place.

"That was foolish. And it changes nothing. But you are correct about my intentions."

Anubis reached into a pocket and brought out a syringe. He pulled the protective cap off with his teeth.

"This will prevent all pain as you die."

Essex writhed and twisted violently to break free. He was helpless against the man's greater strength.

Anubis shoved the needle through Essex's pajamas and into his thigh. Depressed the plunger and injected the contents.

"What's that? Poison?"

"It's a mixture of my own design. It contains curare, Zemuron and Marcaine. It deadens all pain and prohibits all muscle action. And yes, it is strong enough to kill."

"You're insane. Let me go."

"We've gone too far for that. Now just relax. You're about to embark on a wonderful journey. And the most lovely music you've ever heard. Both will be unique to you alone for every person has a different journey into the next dimension. I'm going to join you part way. Perhaps all the way. We'll see. But I assure you there will be no pain. I've tested this formula on many people and nobody has ever complained." Anubis chuckled at his own words.

Essex struggled wildly to break free of Anubis' hold. His struggles rapidly weaken as the drug took effect. They ceased with his hate filled eyes locked on those of Anubis. Essex's mouth worked and a hoarse whisper came from between slack lips.

"You've killed me."

"Yes. That's the truth of it. But I've given you something more beautiful than life. And don't worry about Heaven or Hell for no such places exist. Allow me to explain that to you. The forces of the universe are in a constant state of flux. Out of this flux, the mind of man creates a place of abode for his spirit after the body dies. I've seen the beginning of the journeys men take to this place." Anubis paused and reflected on those scenes, and then continued to speak with regret. "I've never seen the end of a journey. And so I don't know who or what is waiting for them upon their arrival. I do know that you have a grand experience coming."

"Why me?" Essex whispered weakly.

"I search out unique people, especially warriors such as you. And poets, gangsters, adventurers, politicians for these types of men have the most fascinating death dreams. I journey with them into the afterlife to see the pure beauty, to hear the beautiful celestial music that exists there."

Anubis reclined beside Essex and placed his head against the gray one.

Essex's chest rose. Fell. Rose no more.

Abruptly, in another dimension, Anubis stood two steps behind Essex on a white sand beach bordering a dazzling blue ocean. Both men were barefooted and dressed in snow-white seamen's jumpers and trousers. Essex glowed with health.

A light of unbelievable purity bathed this world. The light had no source, seemingly coming from everywhere, and nowhere. Just being. The beach stretched left and right as far as the eye could see. The sand surface was pristine with not one footprint of man or animal marring it. A range of green forested hills lay behind the men a half mile distant.

Grand music performed by a giant, invisible orchestra filled this world. It was a celestial orchestra creating music of total perfection. The gentle wash of the blue waves upon the sandy beach make a delightful musical sound that blended perfectly into the symphony.

A pair of gray sandpipers ran nimble footed along the water's edge. The birds warbled a happy melody in perfect harmony with the music. A great blue heron passed overhead with measured, stately strokes. Each stroke of the long feathered wings was like the stroke of a skilled musician's fingers upon the strings of a cello, the music lovely in timbre and beat. This world held total beauty.

Anubis laughed out loud with joy at the sound of the lovely music and the stupendous beauty of the land and ocean. He caught himself and looked quickly at Essex to see if the man had heard the laugh.

Essex gave no sign that he was conscious of Anubis' presence. He continued to stare out across the blue ocean that merged with the blue sky on the far distant horizon. His face showed his deep love and relish of the sea. He began to hum in a tuneful voice. He was anticipating some coming adventure.

Anubis turned and looked across the ocean in the same direction as Essex. His eyes widen with amazement. He smiled broadly. A sailing ship with two tall masts full of gleaming white sails had appeared on the ocean not half a league distant. Its course was toward the shore. The ships glided along at a speed that seems unnaturally fast for the slow, gentle wind.

A short distance off shore, the ship lowered her sails and dropped anchor. Seamen began lowering a boat into the water. The boat, rowed by two oarsmen and with a coxswain at the tiller, pulled toward the beach. The sailors were dressed in sparkling white uniforms similar to the ones Anubis and Essex wore. Though the oarsmen seemed to be rowing at a leisurely pace, the boat moved swiftly. In but a few seconds, the boat grounded on the beach.

The coxswain, a stoutly built redhead, jumped into the shallow water and waded ashore. He gave Essex a snappy salute and asked, "Sir, are you ready to come aboard?"

"Is the ship prepared for the voyage?"

"Yes, sir. She's in as fine a condition as a ship ever was."

"Then let's go aboard."

Essex stepped into the boat and seated himself in the bow.

Anubis made to follow Essex onto the boat. He progressed a few feet. Then a doubtful expression flooded his face and he halted. He built courage and took another step forward. Halted again. The doubtful expression was more intense. He just couldn't build the courage to board the boat.

Neither the sailors nor Essex looked at Anubis. They gave no indication they were aware of his presence. The coxswain shoved the boat free of the beach, climbed in and again took his place in the stern. He caught hold of the tiller.

"Heave away, lads," the coxswain called.

The oarsmen began to stroke in perfect unison.

Anubis stood on the beach and watched the boat pull away. His expression became one of ever greater anger at himself for not joining Essex on the ship. He smacked a fist into a palm. What grand adventures will he have missed by his caution?

"Next time I WILL go," he whispered out loud.

The boat had moved speedily over the water with little exertion by the oarsmen and was already at the ship. Essex and the seamen climbed the Jacob's ladder and onto the ship. The boat was hoisted aboard and placed on the ship's davits. Men could be seen turning the capstan. The anchor emerged from the water. The ship turned and went off with her sails full of the invisible wind.

As the ship carrying Essex drew away, the clear, radiant light of the day around Anubis dimmed swiftly. The white sand beach turned gray, the sea water black. The grand music, fading rapidly, was but a frail sound, and even that was discordant and jarring. Essex had taken all beauty of this world away with him.

Anubis heard a slight sound behind him and tensed. He spun to give battle with what creature might lurk in this now dimly lighted world.

A very tall, gaunt man, hardly more than a skeleton, stood a few paces away and watching Anubis. If he had meat on his bones, he'd be bigger than Anubis.

The man was dressed all in black, tight fitting trousers, shirt, coat with a long tail, a high crowned hat and leather boots reaching to his knees. His skin was the pale of death, at least what little Anubis could see of it for most was hidden by a bristly black beard and tangled black hair falling onto his shoulders. His nose was a long, high beak rising above a wide slit of a mouth. Large black eyes stared out from deep pits beneath hairy brows.

Skeleton Man's mouth opened into a gaping, toothless hole in the center of that mass of black hair. From the cavernous mouth, a gleeful laughter poured forth at Anubis' cowardly action. Skeleton Man broke into a wild jig, laughing and clapping his hands and whirling about on the sand. Skeleton Man was really enjoying himself at Anubis' expense.

He danced for three seconds. And VANISHED.

Anubis staggered back. He couldn't believe what he had seen. He blinked and stared at the place where the man had stood. He shook his head. Who the hell was that? What the hell was that? Nothing like this had ever happened before. He looked at the sand where the man had danced. The sand was perfectly smooth. Not one footprint. Had he only imagined the apparition?

Anubis nodded to himself. Real or not, the thing was gone. If it came again and sought battle, he would give it more than it wanted.

Around Anubis the last ray of light blinked out as if a great curtain had been drawn and total darkness fell upon this world.

Anubis jerked awake in Essex's bedroom and on the bed beside the body of the admiral. He threw a quick look down at Essex's corpse, with its gray hair glowing silver in the moonlight. Both the admiral and he again wore their regular clothing.

Anubis jumped from the bed and hurried from the room and out of the house.

Chapter Three

The temperature had dropped rapidly and the stiff wind had teeth when Dan reached the subway station. A powerful gust struck him in the back and whipped leaves and scraps of paper down the concrete steps with him as he descended into the underground station. He immediately felt the warmer air of the dimly lit underground station and smelled the dusty, mustiness of the place. He halted at the turnstile and dug for his wallet.

As he fished money from the wallet, he threw a quick look at the subway loading platform close to the rails. A score of men and women stood waiting for a train. Among them was a gaunt young man about Dan's age of late twenties and leaning heavily on a cane. He held three large, framed pictures wrapped with brown paper and bound with a leather strap. Also in the crowd were two tough looking young men wearing loose fitting pants and jackets and billed hats. Their ears were plugged into music and their heads bobbed up and down to the rhythm, like ducks eating bugs from the surface of pond water.

Dan saw the two Bug Eaters pull the ear plugs out and grin at each other. They began to scan the crowd. Dan recognized the intent of the two and it wasn't good, two jackals looking for a weak one among the herd of innocents around them to isolate and bring down.

The crowd came to life and stirred as the iron rattle of an approaching train swept out of the nearby tunnel. The train popped into view and stopped with a squeal of brakes at the station platform. The doors of the coaches slid open and people poured from the train. They dodged the people pushing onto the train, and hurried onward across the station platform toward the exit.

Dan fed money to the ticket machine and pushed on the turnstile. It wouldn't give way to allow him to pass. He checked the train. The last of the passengers were boarding. He wasn't going to make the train if he didn't hurry. He tried the turnstile and again no movement. Time was running out. To hell with paying. He vaulted over the turnstile and sprinted toward the train.

The Man with the cane, carefully shielding his paintings, held back to allow the last person, a woman, to enter the car ahead of him. Which wasn't a good move. As he was about to follow her on board the train, the nearer Bug Eater stepped close and knocked the paintings from his hand.

Cane Man hastily bent to retrieve the pictures. The second Bug Eater kicked him in the ribs and drove him to hands and knees on the concrete platform, and quickly kicked him again in the ribs. The doors swept shut in Cane Man's face and the train sped off.

Cane Man knew he had been chosen for a mugging. He lashed out with his cane at the nearest Bug Eater and caught him a solid wallop across the side of the head. The man backed up, half falling.

The second Bug Eater jumped in and struck Cane Man with a fist and knocked him flat on the concrete. Both Bug Eaters piled on top of the man.

Cane Man fought back strongly, pounding up at the faces of his attackers. He was no match for both men and was receiving twice as many blows as he was giving, and getting a hell of a beating.

Dan, closing fast upon the three men, saw the attack. "Bastards," he growled, and charged upon the three fighters. He grabbed the nearer Bug Eater by the jacket and jerked him off Cane Man, and instantly mashed him in the face with a fist. With the landing of the blow, Dan's face contorted with rage. He held the mugger and gave him a powerful punch to the face, and another, and another, his fist making sodden whacking sounds as knuckles crunched flesh.

Cane Man, lying flat on his back, thrust his hand against the man's chest and shoved him up to arm's length and hammered him with powerful blows of his fist. The mugger went limp. Cane Man shoved him off onto the floor of the station and hastily looked at the Good Samaritan savagely pounding the second mugger, now unconscious. The man gave no sign he was ever going to stop hitting the man.

Cane Man shouted out, "Stop! That's enough! That's enough!"

Dan didn't hear the shout through his anger and kept pounding the mugger's bleeding face.

Still lying on his back, Cane Man snatched up his cane and struck Dan a hard blow across the shanks.

"Stop, damn it," he roared.

The pain of the blow on his leg and the strident cry broke through Dan's lust to savage the man. He stopped his cocked fist and aimed hard blue eyes down at Cane Man.

"Why the hell stop?" he said, scowling. "They deserve a real beating and I'm the man to give it to them."

"Do you want to kill one of them and have to explain that to the police?"

Dan continued to hold the mugger as he considered Cane Man's words. His face lost its fierce expression and he let the unconscious man fall onto the platform.

Dan's expression softened further and he began to chuckle. "Damn, I hate it when someone is more right than I am."

He stepped to Cane Man and extends his hand. "Here. Let me help you up."

Cane Man took hold of the offered hand and Dan pulled him to his feet.

"You all right?" Dan asked, sizing up the crippled man. The fellow was gaunt, face and body. Still he had fought with strength. He was evaluating Dan as keenly as Dan was him. Dan liked the steady eyes of the man.

"Yeah. I've had a lot worse ones."

"So I see," Dan said and glancing at the man's leg. "How'd you get that bum leg?"

"The Marines gave me a three year vacation in Iraq and Afghanistan. Got caught in a bomb blast."

"Spent time there myself with them. But seems I was luckier than you. How's the leg coming?"

"It's healing okay. Should be able to throw this cane away in a couple of weeks."

Dan cast a look toward the entrance, and then chucked a thumb down at the two unconscious men. "Best we hurry and do something with those two sons-of-bitches before someone comes and sees them."

He caught the two would be muggers by the collars of their jackets and dragged them across the platform and up against the side wall of the station. One man came half conscious and groaned. Dan stomped him in the ribs. The man stopped groaning.

Dan positioned the two on their backs and folded their arms across their chest as if they were but sleeping. He nodded satisfied with his work and returned to Cane Man, just as two men came down the steps and into the station.

"What's with the pictures?" Dan asked and gestured at them as Cane Man gathered them up off the station platform.

"They're paintings. Oil paintings."

"Okay. Oil paintings. You the painter?"

"Yeah."

"You're lucky to be able to paint. I can hardly write my name. You paint them for yourself or to sell?"

"I paint to sell. Though I'm going to keep one of these."

"Sounds like you're onto something." Dan cocked an ear toward the tunnel. "Here comes a train. You ready to travel?"

"The sooner we're away from here the better."

The train burst from the tunnel and halted. Dan and Cane Man entered the half full train and found seats together. The train sped off rattling and swaying.

Dan held out his hand. "I'm Dan Gallatin."

Cane Man took the offered hand and clasped it firmly. "Ethan Sommers. Thanks for the help back there. I wasn't doing so good."

"No thanks needed. I believe you would've done the same for me." Dan nodded at the paintings. "How about showing me how good you are?"

"Sure, why not." Ethan began to remove the strap holding the paintings.

"What're they about?"

"Women and war."

"Well hell yes, what else is there."

Ethan leaned his cane against a leg and unwrapped the paintings and offered one to Dan, who positioned it to catch as much illumination as possible from the light of the subway car. The painting showed a bomb blasted Humvee on a Baghdad street. Smoke rose from the mutilated machine. The body of a Marine lay on the shattered pavement near the twisted open door of the machine. The Marine had no legs. A second Marine all broken and bleeding and showing great pain lay close by the first. An Iraqi man stood looking down at the Marines. The man showed no emotion, he could have been looking at a rock.

Dan returned the painting and accepted a second and then a third. Both were of beauty. One showed an exceedingly lovely young woman standing on the shore of a high mountain lake. The lake waters were calm as glass and reflected a few puffs of clouds in a blue sky and the forested mountain on the far side of the lake. The last one was a close-up of the same lovely young woman. Her innocence and gentle expression made Dan's heart thump. He was captivated by the girl's features, by Ethan's portrayal of them.

"Damn fine work, Ethan."

"Thanks."

"I'd like to meet a girl like that. She real?"

"Very real. She's one of the tonics that keeps my head half way straight."

"I could stand that kind of a tonic."

"You got some real bruises there on your knuckles. You didn't get all of them from that one little tussle back there."

Dan lifted his hands and examined the knuckles showing old scars, and fresh bruises forming bloody scabs.

"Nope. Had a prize fight a little while ago. I earn my money in a different way than you."

"You win?"

"I'd be in damn worse condition if I hadn't."

"How'd you come to be a fighter?"

"Tried it out in the Marine Corps and found I was good at it. And it's quick money. But not easy money for someone could get in a lucky punch and scramble my brains."

"I saw your face when you were hitting that fellow. You like to hit people?"

"If somebody crowds me, I give him a few licks."

"Or you give him a lot of licks."

Dan scowled at that. "Sometimes that too. And it doesn't feel bad doing it either."

"How about when they hit you back?"

"That's all right if I'm giving more than I'm getting. But that doesn't happen very often."

"Were you like that before being over there?"

"I got mad quick. But I didn't hit people."

"Everybody was changed by the fighting," Ethan said. "Your mind gets screwed up by the constant fear of being blown all to hell by a roadside bomb, or a sniper sending one through you, or entering a house that might be booby-trapped."

Ethan paused, remembering things of the past. "Damn near everyone could use some help in adjusting back to civilian life. But I don't believe anybody is ever totally healed from the stress of not knowing if this patrol was the one where he was going to die."

"I hated riding the streets worse than I did the firefights," Dan said. "Those damn roadside bombs could blow your balls off and then you'd have nothing to live for. In the fire fights you knew where the enemy was and you got to shoot back and try to kill him."

"But this thing about your tonics. You said you had two kinds for keeping your head straight. What's the second one after the girl?"

"A visit with Colonel Granville. Most of the men call him Colonel Dream Maker."

Dan cocked an eye at Ethan. "Colonel Dream Maker? That's a damn strange name. Must be a story that goes with it."

"He was my colonel. He knows firsthand what it was like over there. He's helped me clear my head and probably could yours too."

"He's a psychiatrist?"

"No, not a psychiatrist. I'd say he's something much better. He's good for all the men, but he's really best for the men who lost an arm or leg in the fighting."

Ethan studied Dan for a moment. "Say, I've got an idea if you got a couple of hours. Why not come with me to one of his meetings. There's one tonight."

Dan considered the offer but a moment. "Sure. I got time. No work tonight."

"Where do you work."

"At the Bank Vault Club."

"I've heard of it. Country western club. Rough place I've been told."

"Used to be. But not anymore. I'm the bouncer there now and I put a quick stop to any rough stuff."

Ethan looked at Dan's hands. "That should give you a lot of chances to use your fists."

Dan's face hardened with quick anger. He raised his clenched fists and looked over them at Ethan. "These fists kept you from getting your ass stomped into the concrete," he said testily.

"Hey. Hold up." Ethan said and gave Dan a toothy smile. "You wouldn't hit a cripple, would you?"

Dan lowered his fist with a sheepish grin. "Maybe not this time."

"Good. We'll stop off at my place first and I'll drop off these paintings."

"What's the story of this colonel being called Dream Maker?"

"You won't believe me. Just wait and see for yourself. You've got a real surprise coming."

Chapter Four

Dan and Ethan, with Ethan leading, entered the huge meeting hall of the Veterans of Foreign Wars on Carrington Street. Ethan carried a rolled blanket under his arm. They halted just inside and cast a look around.

Dan judged the hall contained at least a hundred veterans. They ran the gamut of ages, from young men to gray beards with deeply creased faces. Most of them were dressed in casual clothing. A score or so wore some article of military uniform. A few of the vets were dressed in expensive business suits. More than a score leaned on crutches or canes. Half that number sat in wheelchairs.

In a back corner of the hall, men in tattered, dirty clothing, men who lived on the streets, stood separated and isolated from the better dressed vets. One of the street men coughed raggedly. He hastily covered his mouth with a dirty hand and looked guiltily around.

Here and there a pair of men talked in subdued voices. Most men stood or sat alone, silent, turned inward to private thoughts and emotions.

Dan sensed tenseness in the men. The vets were obviously waiting for something important to happen. Frequent looks were thrown at the small stage in the far end of the hall.

The hall was bare of furniture except for the three chairs on the stage. The floor directly in front of the stage was covered with folded blankets and other pieces of cloth lined up in neat, straight rows. Like men in military ranks. Each cloth was large enough for a man to lie upon.

"I didn't expect to see so many vets here," Dan said. "And some of them are eighty, even ninety years old. They must have served in World War II."

"That's right. If you count all the vets of all the wars, there has to be tens of thousands of them in Chicago."

"This place looks like a Muslim mosque, what with all the rugs spread out like that."

"They're not prayer rugs."

"I didn't think they were."

"However there may be a few Muslims here, the colonel doesn't exclude anyone that wants to come to one of his sessions."

"He has a good turnout. How often does he hold these sessions?"

"Three or four times a week. He holds them at several places around town to make it easier for vets to get to them."

"What does he do for them? And why?"

"As to why, you'll have to ask him yourself. But I believe he does it because somebody should help the damaged warriors and he can. As to what, you'll soon see for yourself. There he comes now."

Dan turned to look. A door had opened behind the stage and Marine Colonel Granville in full uniform had entered the room. His left chest carried no medals. A uniformed Marine sergeant accompanied the colonel. His chest was also without medals. The sergeant wore a Marine issue pistol on his side. The colonel stopped and looked out from the stage and upon the throng of men.

"Why the armed sergeant?" Dan asked. "He acts like a bodyguard."

"The sergeant and his gun showed up about two weeks ago. He served with the colonel in Iraq same as I did. He's one tough fellow. The colonel believes someone is stalking him."

"Some freaked out vet?"

"Not according to the colonel. But I don't know much about it for he just barely mentioned it. Let me introduce you to him. Now don't be surprised at what you see."

Ethan and Dan made their way through the vets in front of them to Colonel Granville standing on the stage. He turned and looked down at Ethan and Dan as they halt.

Dan was startled at the appearance of the Colonel's face. It was scarred as if the skin had been fried, and there were no eyebrows, no eyelashes. His eyes were unbelievable, the orbs totally covered with scores of tiny crystals that now made up the cornea. The crystals sparkled as if charged with electricity. Looking past the colonel's face, Dan saw that, though a large man, the colonel had a weariness, a frailness about him.

The Colonel aimed his crystal studded eyes down at Ethan. "Hello, Ethan" he said. "Good to see you again."

"You too, colonel. I'd like you to meet a friend of mine. Name's Dan Gallatin."

Colonel turned his face toward Dan and put his hand out. This man with the strange eyes knew exactly where Dan and Ethan were standing.

"It's a pleasure to meet you, Dan," said the colonel in a strong voice.

Dan shook the offered hand, a firm hand with a warmth to it.

"Hello, Colonel Granville."

Granville held his crystalline eyes on Dan and studied him intently. After a moment he spoke, "I see that you are surprised by my appearance."

"Yes, sir. I've never seen eyes like yours before."

"Truthful and to the point. I like that." The colonel continued to study Dan.

Behind Dan came the rising voices of the vets eager for whatever was coming.

"We must have a talk one day soon. But for now, the men are growing impatient to receive what they have gathered here for."

Ethan nudged Dan. "Let's find a spot to spread the blanket." He led off.

Dan followed Ethan to a vacant spot in the rear of the room, where Ethan quickly spread the blanket he had carried. He sat down upon the blanket and motioned Dan down beside him. "Get ready for a new adventure," Ethan said, his voice holding a boyish eagerness.

The other veterans, those not in wheelchairs, were hastily seating themselves upon the floor cloths they had brought. Those vets of the street fanned out along the rear wall and lay down upon the floor.

Visible now to Dan was a young woman, in her mid twenties he judged, wearing a Marine fatigue jacket over black slacks. She was placing a strip of rug on the floor just inside the door. She appeared weary, her face pale, holding a drawn, even a haunted expression with the skin tight over the bones beneath.

Dan turned to the colonel who was staring out at the crowd. The colonel called out in a gentle voice, "Young woman there in the back. Would you please leave?"

"No, I won't leave," said the woman in a firm voice and straightened to stand very erect. "I'm a vet and I've seen combat. I've heard about you and I could use some help to stop my headaches and bad dreams."

"I can see that you're a vet," replied the colonel, "but this session is for men and wouldn't be proper for you."

"Let me be the judge of that," the woman said, her tone even more unyielding.

"I would like to do that." The colonel's voice held a patient tone. "But the men will ask for dreams that I know wouldn't be acceptable to a woman."

A man jumped up from his blanket near Kristin and grabbed her by the shoulder. "You're wasting our time," he said angrily. "Get out like the colonel said."

The man spun the woman around and shoved her toward the door. She jerked free and thrust the man away.

"I'm not leaving," she cried out angrily. "Now keep your damn hands off me."

"You sure as hell are," said the man, and moved to take hold of the woman again.

Dan exploded up from his blanket and stepped in between the man and woman. He stiff armed the man and stopped him dead in his tracks.

"Easy, fellow. No rough stuff with the girl."

The man swung a quick fist at Dan. Who blocked the blow and glared threateningly at the man.

"You try that again and I'll knock your face to the back of your head."

"You three soldiers, stand at attention!" the colonel's order came sharply across the hall.

Dan, the man, and the woman came to stiff attention and froze there.

The colonel continued to speak. "Now young lady, you've caused enough disturbance. I'll meet with you after this is over. Gallatin, please escort her outside."

Dan turned and offered his arm to the woman. "Allow me, miss," he said and gave her a pleasant gentleman's smile.

The woman's angry expression relaxed as she looked across the hall to the colonel. "All right, colonel. I'll leave for now. I'll be waiting."

She turned to Dan with his arm extended. "I don't need that," she said, her tone soft to lessen the impact of the rejection. She fell into step beside Dan and they walked from the hall.

They halted outside the door and she turned and looked into Dan's eyes. "Thanks for standing up for me. But I can take care of myself."

"I'm sure you can. But this allowed me to be a hero."

Dan liked her low, husky voice, though it had been strong when she had talked with the colonel. She was almost as tall as Dan, slender and very fair. Her face was finely chiseled, her nose straight, mouth a little large. She was bareheaded, and her black hair was being tousled by the wind on the street. He liked looking into her eyes, green in color he thought but couldn't be sure in the night and the light of the distant streetlight striking them weakly.

"Nothing that the colonel would have done would've shocked me. I've seen about everything there is to see."

"I'm sure the colonel knows best." Dan looked steadily at her. "What's your name?"

"Kristin Goodfolk," she said and held out her hand.

Dan took her hand and found it chilled. "I'm Dan Gallatin. Glad to meet you Kristin."

"You too, Dan."

"Now I better get back inside and see what's happening."

Kristin focused on Dan. "Goodbye, hero," she said and gave him a small smile.

Dan noted the smile removed part of Kristin's haunted look. He looked closely at her, evaluating the curve of her lips, the shape and color of her eyes, the press of her bosom against the man's shirt she wore. She could be very pretty in other situations.

"Goodbye," he said, returned her smile.

He pivoted about and re-entered the hall and seated himself on the blanket beside Ethan.

The colonel called out in a strong voice to the throng of veterans. "Men, what would you like tonight?"

Many men called out suggestions, their voices overriding each other.

A man on crutches shouted out. "I want to run again. Run fast through some place really beautiful."

A very old man with white hair and sitting in a wheelchair laughed and added, "Hell. I'd be satisfied to walk again. Make me walk, colonel."

A third man shouted out, "Give me a woman. A pretty, willing one with nice soft hips."

A street man shivered and pulled his thin coat more tightly around himself. "Give me something to look at beside these dirty Chicago streets. And for God's sake, some place where it's warm."

"Why not all of those things?" said the colonel, and he smiled. If the grotesque grimace on that disfigured face could be called a smile. His crystal covered eyes had come alive with a brilliant light. He seemed suddenly to be charge with energy.

The veterans filled the hall with a great shout of approval. The walls vibrated with their voices. Then they hastily fell silent as their impatience for what had been promised surged to the front.

"Just relax, close your eyes and listen to the colonel," Ethan said to Dan. "He'll take you to an amazing place."

"If you say so," Dan replied doubtfully, and focused his attention on the colonel. He cocked an ear to listen.

"Listen to me." The colonel's voice was strong, yet gentle. Pausing between each instruction, he continued, "Listen to me. Listen closely to me. You are in a meadow full of beautiful yellow flowers. The meadow is surrounded by tall mountains. A. brook of crystal clear water runs through the meadow. Giant trees in full foliage line the stream. A warm breeze bends the flowers and stirs the leaves of the trees. You are running across the meadow behind a beautiful young woman . . ."

Dan abruptly found himself in a meadow full of yellow daisies. He was chasing after a lovely woman with a mane of red hair flowing on the wind. She wore a red dress the same color as her hair. She was the perfect woman, beautiful, luscious and vibrant with life and it all showed as she ran ahead of him across the meadow with the daisies caressing her gorgeous legs. She turned her lovely face over a shoulder and laughed at Dan. Her expression said, you can have what you can catch. She motioned for him to come to her. She looked back to the front and sped away nimbly over the meadow.

Dan laughed and increased his pace. He enjoyed the chase and intended to catch the prize waiting for him at the end.

The young woman reached the tree lined brook. Crossed it with splashing steps and turned to the left to run beside it.

Dan veered to the side and hurried along the diagonal to the woman's path and gained on her. He leapt across the brook and was only a few steps behind the woman. He overtook her beneath one of the trees, caught her by the shoulders and stopped her flight. He pulled her down in the shade and kissed her gently on the lips, cheeks, neck. She kissed him back through laughter.

They pulled apart and removed their clothes in a leisurely fashion. And all the time they smiled and laughed at each other as if all this was but natural. They made love gently and slowly, extending the length of time their bodies were joined together so as to reap the most pleasure. As the brook rippled musically at their feet and the leaves overhead rustled with a pleasant musical sound.

They pulled apart and lay silently side by side, looking up at the sky. After a time of silence, the woman sat up and pulled Dan's head onto her lap. She began to stroke his face with her finger tips. He looked up into her eyes and smiled and took hold of a length of her thick, red hair.

The woman gave him a sad look and a sob escaped her. Tears welled up from their little salt springs, and pooling in her eyes, overflowed and coursed down her cheeks and fell upon Dan's face. One landed upon his lips.

"What's the mat . . ."

Dan jerked awake and opened his eyes. He was back in the veteran's hall, and surprised at the suddenness of the transition back to the here and now. He licked his lips, tasting for tears.

He heard noises all about him and sat up and looked about. Other vets were awakening from their dreams and glancing about as they oriented themselves to the present.

Dan looked for the colonel. The man was sitting slumped in a chair on the stage and gazing out at the throng of veterans. He appeared exhausted. Dan turned to Ethan sitting on the blanket beside him.

"How do you feel, old soldier?" Ethan asked.

"Just fine. A hell of a dream."

"Was she pretty?"

"Damn. Wasn't she though? So the colonel is a hypnotist and can make a roomful of men dream."

"Do you think that's all he is?"

"What else could he be?"

"See what you think in a day or so. Check back over your experiences in Iraq and Afghanistan and see if they have the same impact on you. I know my memories of all the killing, the bombings, the fear when out on patrol, have lost some of their power to give me nightmares."

"I'm not putting the colonel's dreams down. Dreams are the method by which the human brain sorts through past events and emotions and decides which are important to our survival, and which are harmful. The harmful ones are discarded so that we can function in a logical manner when awake."

Ethan cocked an eye at Dan. "Now where did you pick that up?"

"Read it somewhere." Dan looked toward the stage. Then back at Ethan. "The colonel's leaving."

"Keeping his appointment with the girl I'd bet. I've never known him to break it."

"He seems barely able to walk. Tell me what you know about him."

"He was wounded in Afghanistan. After getting home he started a business downtown where he has an office and does consulting work for several companies. I don't know what kind, but he's made a ton of money. The most sad thing about the colonel is that he was going to resign from the Marines and join NASA. Become an astronaut. Said he wanted to go to the stars, to Alpha Centauri with its two red dwarf suns in orbit around each other."

"How was he injured? How did he get those eyes?"

"He was looking the wrong way when a bomb went off and blew him fifty feet and damn near broke every bone in his body. The flash burned his face and did that terrible thing to his eyes. He once told me that even though he's blind in the normal sense, he can see the electrical coronas that humans produce and that surrounds them, that all living things give off. He said human coronas have the most vivid colors of all of them.

"They're called auras. I've never seen one. But wish I could."

"Right. Auras. I think the colonel can read people's character by the strength and color of their auras. And can mostly read their thoughts too."

"If that's true, then he could be an advisor to some big corporation and make a heap of money telling them what the competition was thinking, what they were up to."

"I'd say so. You ready to catch a train? I know a place that has the best food in town. It's cheap too."

"I am damn hungry. Let's go."

* * * * *

Dan followed Ethan into the small Italian restaurant not far from the hall. He noted some of the veterans had the same urge for food. The kind of exercise the colonel dreamed up for them made a man hungry.

They found seats in a booth and ordered spaghetti and meat balls. They drank beers while they waited for the food.

"Did you notice anything strange during your dream?" Dan asked.

"Like what?"

"Like how the girl acted. Was she sad or happy at the end of the dream. You did have a girl same as me, didn't you?"

Ethan nodded. "Sure I had a girl. But I didn't notice anything strange. I was feeling pretty relaxed there at the end. Did you see anything strange about yours?"

"She was crying."

"Crying? You're not joshing me?"

"No. She had the saddest face. And I heard her crying and I saw tears. Hell, I even tasted them."

"Now, Dan, don't get carried away with your dream. And that's all that it was. Just a dream. She was merely a character in it that you and

Colonel Dream Maker created. Mostly that you created. And sure as hell, nothing more."

"I wouldn't create a girl so sad that she cried. And I don't think the colonel would either. He'd want something to lift the spirits of the vets."

Ethan studied Dan for a moment. "Yeah, that'd be the colonel."

"Maybe there's another answer. You told me that the colonel added something else to the dreams, something that helped vets overcome what bothered them from what they did and what happened to them over there. Maybe he's connected us with something else. Something that's more real than you think. Something even more real than what he thinks."

Ethan shook his head and gave Dan a disbelieving look. "I tell you that she was just a character in your dream."

"Or was she real and I was merely a character in her dream. Or were we both dreaming and for a brief time our dreams connected. Hell, we both might be just part of somebody else's dream."

"Ease up, old boy. You're about to go off the deep end."

Dan frowned as he considered the meaning of what he had said. Then he gave Ethan a grin. "You're most likely right. But the next time you dream with the colonel, don't get so relaxed. See how the other person, the other people in your dream are acting. Try to figure out what they're really thinking."

"OK, Dan, I will. But don't read too much into your dreams. I don't want you to get crazy ideas and run off the track."

Chapter Five

The Bank Vault Club was a rowdy country-western club in South Chicago. It really once was a bank. The bank had failed and the building sold. The partitions had been ripped out to open up a large clear space. The fine hardwood flooring had been kept and made a fine surface upon which to dance. The aged vault with its massive steel door occupied a place of honor in the wall facing the entrance where it would be the first thing people saw upon entering.

Though the night was early, the club was crowded with men and women dressed in western clothing, wide brimmed hats, brightly colored shirts, jeans and boots. A five-piece band on a raised dais played music loud enough to make the crystals tinkle in the big chandelier hanging over the dance floor. Every table was full, except those temporarily vacated by the dancing couples swinging and stomping their booted feet in rhythm to the music. Patrons were jammed shoulder to shoulder at the bar.

Someone has a money-making machine here. That was Ray, the 300 pound fat man serving drinks from behind the long oak bar.

Dan, the peacekeeper, sat at a table near the entrance. He was dressed in jeans, gray cotton shirt and western boots. A book lay open in front of him. A pad of paper and a pencil were close at hand and now and again he made notes from the book.

Dan raised his head from the book and scanned the noisy, rocking crowd. There could be troublemakers here and he wanted to spot them before they started their act. As he evaluated the men, one of the barmaids, small, cute Clara, came up with a tray of drinks. She was dressed in a bright red halter and matching red skirt, so short that it showed a goodly portion of her round, white bottom. Alligator boots enclose her small feet. Clara gave Dan a wink and a bright smile. She plopped down a full mug and took the old one and placed it on her tray.

"More fresh tea with a lot of ice and a touch of lemon just the way you like it," she said.

Dan gave Clara a big brother's smile. "Thanks Clara. Anybody giving you trouble?" She was too young to be working in a place like the Bank Vault, was Dan's judgment.

"Nothing more than a pat on the fanny. And that's all right for it gets me bigger tips."

Dan wasn't happy with the answer. "Just let me know if it gets too friendly."

"I see you're hard at studying. Big test coming up?"

"Yeah. First thing tomorrow."

"How much more college do you need to get your degree?"

"For my doctorate, maybe two more years. And that's if my thesis is accepted."

"Damnation, Dan. You're going to be an old man by that time. What kind of a doctor will you be?"

"A neuroscientist," Dan said and laughed.

"What in the hell is a neuroscientist?"

"It's all about studying the brain, how it works, what parts does what to make us function. How and why it stops working correctly. I'd really like to know how memories are made and stored for a lifetime. And, Clara, I'm not going to be so old. Maybe thirty."

"Before you get too old to do it, you should take me home with you. Or come home with me."

Dan thoughtfully rubbed his chin and pretended to be studying the proposition.

"I'll give that some serious thought."

"That's what you always say. But I'm going to keep asking, for one of these days, you're going to weaken and say yes."

"Hello, Dan," a loud shout sounded out above the rumble of voices in the club.

Dan turned to look in the direction of the call. Paul, a gaunt, hollowed eyed man, and Casey, his pretty girl friend, were winding a course among the tables toward him. Paul was unsteady on his feet and Casey held him tightly by the arm. Both raised a hand and waved at Dan.

Dan came to his feet and called out, "Hello yourself. Come and have a seat before you fall down."

Smiling broadly, Paul and Casey drew near Dan. He gave Casey a hug.

"Don't hug my girl too tight," Paul said, laughing.

"I couldn't take her away from you," Dan said and held out his hand to Paul. He liked the man. "What are you doing here?"

Paul didn't take the offered hand. He stepped close and caught Dan by the shoulders and leaned drunkenly on him. He looked into Dan's face. "We came to see my old war buddy. Ain't that right, Casey?"

Casey nodded and made a sad, frail smile.

"I'm glad you did," Dan said. "But are you sure that you're sober enough to actually see me?"

"I can see just fine, old buddy." Paul said with a drunken grin. "And I'm ready to guard your back just like I did over there."

"You did a damn fine job of it too."

Paul squeezed Dan's shoulders. "You bet your sweet ass I did. And you did the same for me. Yes sir, the same for me too."

Casey took Paul by the arm and drew him away from Dan to stand by her. She retained a firm hold on his arm to help him stand erect.

"Lean on me, honey instead of Dan. It looks better that way."

"I don't give a damn how it looks. Me and old Dan are the best goddamn buddies in the whole goddamn world. Did I ever tell you about the time he . . ."

Yes, you did, honey." Casey interrupted quickly.

"Paul, it looks to me like it's time for you to hit the sack," Dan said.

Paul blinked drunkenly at Dan and leaned more heavily on Casey. "You might just be right. But it's one of those nights when things feel weird. You know, like something is coming down on us. I had to come make sure you were safe."

"Thanks for coming to check on me, but we're all safe. And you've got Casey for company. I'm sure she'll stay with you tonight."

Paul turned and stared at Casey. "She's sure one damn fine beauty. Now ain't she?"

"The most beautiful girl in this whole damn club."

Paul continued to stare into Casey's eyes. "Will you make love to me tonight?"

"Sure, honey, if you want to."

"I've never failed to get it up for you, have I?"

"No. You've always been my stout man."

"Damn right. Damn right. Always ready to go. Never failed."

"Honey, let's go to my place."

Paul turned to Dan. "Her sweet words have seduced me, Dan. So I've got to go with her. She helps me to sleep."

"She's a good one, all right," Dan said.

"I'll take care of him," Casey said and draped one of Paul's arms across her shoulders.

She smiled and nodded to Dan. Then supporting Paul, she moved with him toward the exit.

With a worried expression, Dan watched after the pair.

Clara came and stood by Dan's side as she too watched Paul and Casey leave.

"Your friend sure has a load on," she said.

"Yes he does. Makes him look stupid. But he's the most intelligent man I've ever seen. In fact, he's too intelligent for his own good."

"What do you mean?"

"He has one of those minds that remembers everything he sees and hears. And he's been in some hellish stuff. It keeps replaying over and over in his head."

"You saw the same stuff? Didn't you?'

"Yeah. But my memory of it is gradually fading. Just not fast enough."

"You're worried about him?"

"I think I'll take him to see the colonel."

"Who?"

"Colonel Dream Maker. One day, I'll tell you about him."

"I'd like to hear about him."

Clara winked at Dan. "Well back to business." She pranced off in her alligator boots. She swished her round, tantalizing hips back at Dan as she moved away.

Dan shook his head and grinned. He seated himself and lowered his eyes back to the book, titled, 'Effects Of Anesthesia Upon The Brain'.

BANG! The ugly crack of exploding gunpowder slashed through the din of music and voices in the Bank Vault. Clara screamed. Her tray of drinks fell from her hands to the floor with a crash and clatter.

Dan instantly sprang to his feet and scanned the room, looking for Clara. She was clutching her crotch with both hands. She swept her frightened eyes around. The found Dan and locked upon him.

"OH, my God! Dan, I've been shot! Help me!" She cried out in a voice filled with pain.

Dan sprinted toward Clara, shoving aside men and women who had sprung to their feet and were blocking his way. He saw Ray, holding his 9mm pistol, come out from behind the bar and charge like a speeding tank toward the trouble.

Dan reached Clara and wrapped her protectively in his arms. Just as Ray lumbered up. The big man pivoted his massive body and put it into a protective screen for Dan and Clara.

Dan's hard eyes searched the faces of the men and women at the nearby tables. They all register startled expressions. Except for one table where three men still sat. Two pf the men were laughing and watching the third who was grimacing with pain and blowing on his fingers.

Dan looked down at the floor close around the man with the hot fingers. The shredded paper of an exploded firecracker littered the floor. Dan knew instantly what had happened and red hot anger surged through him. He released Clara and leapt upon Firecracker Man, jerked the man to his feet and twisted his right arm up behind his back, way up high until it was ready to tear from its socket. The man screamed.

"You sonofabitch!" Dan hissed into the man's face.

Ray quickly stepped to the table and pointed the 9mm into the faces of the seated men. He aimed a savage look down at the two. "Goddamn you for hurting one of my girls. If you move, I'll blast you into next week."

Dan shook Firecracker Man. "This one put a firecracker up under Clara's skirt and let it go off."

"Damn bastard. Do what's right with him, Dan. I'll see that these two stay good boys."

Holding Firecracker Man's arm pinned behind, Dan emptied the man's pockets out on the table. Among the bills and change and pocketknife, were two firecrackers. Dan looked at Clara, who was being comforted by another bargirl. Tears of pain and anger streaked Clara's face. Her hands were still between her legs and cradling her private parts.

"Clara, are you up to helping me with a little job?"

A hard, pitiless smile overrode Clara's pain. She wanted revenge on the man in the most awful way.

"If it's to make that bastard hurt, then you bet I am."

"Good. Take those two firecrackers and twist their fuses together and light them."

Clara glared at Firecracker Man. "You're the lowest fucker I've ever seen. I'm going to love this."

Clara released her hold on her crotch and snatched up the firecrackers. Swiftly she twisted the fuses together, whipped out a Zippo from a little pocket in her skirt and thumbed it into flame. She touched the fuses and they burned with a hiss of red fire.

Dan grabbed the waist of Firecracker Man's pants and tore them open wide enough to allow Clara's hand to slide down inside.

"Put them in there," he directed.

Clara jammed the firecrackers down in the man's pants and hurriedly jerked her hand out.

The two firecrackers exploded with the sound of a large caliber pistol. The front of Firecracker Man's pants bulged. Smoke billowed out the waist. The man shrieked with pain.

"God, I love to hear that," Clara said, smiling hugely.

"Dan, I think he's on fire," Ray said.

Dan leisurely picked up a mug of beer from a nearby table and sloshed it down into the man's trousers. "That should put it out. Now stop your bellowing."

"Let's give them the rush," Ray said.

Dan caught Firecracker Man by the collar and the seat of his pants. He pulled the man's pants up so tightly into the crack of his ass that he was walking on tiptoes as Dan hustled him toward the exit of the club.

Ray, prodding the other two men with his 9mm, followed close behind Dan.

Dan shoved the door of the Bank Vault open with Firecracker Man's body, and flung the man sprawling on hands and knees onto the sidewalk. As Ray appeared through the door with the other two men, Dan grabbed each one and sent him crashing down onto the concrete.

Firecracker Man rose slowly to his feet. He rubbed his half dislocated arm and shoulder and glared at Dan. His mouth worked with anger. "I bet that little whore won't be spreading her legs for a man any time soon."

Firecracker man should have kept his mouth shut for Dan went ballistic. He hurled himself upon the man and smashed him in the face, twice, pile driver blows, and hammered him down unconscious to the sidewalk. That punishment sure as hell wasn't enough. Dan cocked his size 12 boot to stomp the man in the face.

"Dan, no law suits," Ray shouted and reached for Dan to halt him.

Dan controlled himself with a huge effort. Slowly, reluctantly he lowered his foot. He turned to the other two men.

"I think your stupid friend needs some help to walk. Now pick him up and get out of my sight. If I ever see either of you three here again, I'm going to beat you like no man has ever been beaten before."

The two men speedily caught Firecracker Man under the arms and carried him off with his feet dragging on the sidewalk.

For the first time, Dan noted a sedan had pull up in front of the club and the occupants were watching him. In the back seat were Ethan and Colonel Granville. The Marine sergeant was in front as driver.

Ethan opened the rear door and climbed out and stood on the sidewalk. "Hello, Dan," he said.

"Hello, Ethan," Dan replied. "You missed out on some fireworks."

"Seems like I just saw some."

"I didn't mean that kind. You come for some entertainment and a drink?"

"Sounds good, but no." He nodded at the car. "The colonel wants to have a talk with you. You got time for a little ride?"

"Sure. Things are quiet now." He spoke to Ray. "You'll take care of Clara?"

"You know I will."

"Then I'll see you in a little while."

Ray gave the men a nod and walked toward the door of the Club.

Ethan motioned at the rear seat of the vehicle. "In the back with the colonel, if you will. I'll ride up front with the sergeant."

Dan climbed into the vehicle, noting as he did so, that Colonel Granville was dressed in civilian clothing. So too was the sergeant.

Ethan took the passenger seat and then twisted about so that he could see Dan and Colonel Granville. The sergeant started the car and drove off along the night street.

"Good to see you again, Dan," said the colonel.

"You too, colonel. What's up?"

"Thanks for giving me some of your time."

"That's about all I've got."

"Maybe we can fix that."

Dan gave the colonel a sharp look. "How so?"

"Ethan told me about the trouble in the subway. Since then, I've spent the day having you checked out. I know that you are attending the university and studying to be a neuroscientist, and about your bare knuckle fighting in the cages on the waterfront. If I have read you correctly, I believe you're the fellow for a proposition I have."

"I'm willing to listen."

"Ethan has told you that I'm being stalked. Actually it's more than that. I believe a man plans to kill me."

"Do you know who?"

"No, and I don't know why. If I did then I might be able to figure out who he was."

"Do you think it could be somehow related to your ability to make men dream," Dan asked.

"That was my first thought. But even if that is true, it hasn't helped me to know who he is."

"Have you seen him?"

"In my way of seeing, yes. But before we get into that, do you believe humans have an aura? And each one has a color and intensity different from all others?"

"I've never seen one. But I wouldn't rule it out since our bodies are a chemical and electrical engine. Electrical impulses are constantly rushing around our bodies. Our brain is an electrical powerhouse. And we know electrical currents give off an electromagnetic field around them. And burning objects give off heat which can be felt, and can be seen with the right ability."

The colonel nodded. "I can see every person's aura very clearly. With my adjusted vision." He laughed mockingly at his words.

"A child's aura is a beautiful thing with the pure, bright color of innocence. The color of auras darken as people age and accumulate varying degrees of sorrow, misgivings, even hate and murder." The colonel paused. "This man stalking me has murdered people. Murdered many times I believe. And I know he intends to kill me. I've done nothing against him. I don't even know his name. Where he lives. Nothing."

Dan spoke. "You said you've seen him."

"Yes, two times on the street our cars passed close and I saw him. He looked directly at me. I sensed his thoughts the same as I sense yours now, that you don't fully believe me."

Dan allowed the remark about his disbelief go past without comment. "If he plans to kill you, why is he letting you see him?"

"He's obviously playing with me for some reason only he knows."

The sergeant suddenly spun the steering wheel of the car and made a sharp U-turn in the middle of the block and pulled quickly to the curb and parked. He intently watched the cars passing on the street.

The sergeant looked at the colonel. "Just making sure we weren't being followed, colonel."

"Right."

The men sat silently and watched the traffic flow past. No car slowed or turned.

"Nothing, colonel," said the sergeant. He shifted into gear and drove back into the line of traffic heading back toward the Bank Vault Club.

"What do you want from me?" Dan asked the colonel.

"Find this man for me."

"Why not have the police try to find him," Dan said with some surprise.

"I have nothing concrete to give them to work on. Just the suspicion of a man that most everybody thinks is blind. And mostly is. They'd not waste time on my complaint."

"You're most likely right. How about hiring a private detective? He'd be better at this sort of thing than me. Or have the sergeant do this? Or Ethan?"

"I've considered all of that. I don't want a detective involved. As for Ethan and the sergeant, they're both brave and trustworthy men.

However your study of the human brain and mind makes you the logical person to do this. My strange vision that allows me to see auras must interest you. And you must be wondering why this man stalks me. All this has to appeal to your curiosity."

"It does, and that's a fact. But I don't have the time. I work for a living and need every penny I can earn for my tuition at the college and for living expenses."

The Colonel taps himself on the chest. Runs his hand over his scarred face. "This body of mine is pretty beat up and has a lot of aches and pain. But it's the only one I've got and I'd like to keep blood flowing through it. So I'm willing to pay to keep someone from stopping it from running. If you do this, I'll pay for all of your tuition and living expenses for a year."

"What? You're talking about maybe forty grand."

"I know and I'm willing to pay it. And with a little bargaining from you, I might increase the payment. Now before you say anything more, I must tell you again that this man has murdered people. By the color of his aura, I believe many people. The job will be very dangerous and you'll earn your money. Every cent of it."

Dan looked out at the night, the traffic whizzing past and the tall buildings looming high against the sky. The job somehow appealed to him. Also the colonel said a little negotiating could mean more money. How much could that be? Dan would test the colonel?

"You may have thought of another factor to the proposition," said the colonel. "It could turn out that you will be forced into a situation where you would have to fight for your life. Even to kill the man."

"Yes, that did come to mind." Dan said, and remembering the men he had killed to stay alive, and to keep his Marine buddies alive. This wasn't so much different, except the pay now could be a hell of a lot greater.

He faced back to the colonel. "Two years of tuition and living expenses."

Colonel Granville hesitated but a moment. "Yes, that is the length of time you will need to complete your degree. I agree for I know the odds are high that you will likely have to kill the man when he comes looking for you."

Dan was surprised at the quick agreement with his counteroffer. "Since we don't know anything about him, do you have a suggestion how I do it?"

"You start stalking me. Or rather you act like you are."

Dan broke into laughter. "Why hell yes. Let the bastard spot me slipping around and spying on you. He'll see me as an obstacle to his plan, whatever it is, and try to get rid of me. When he comes at me, that'll give me a chance to find out who he is."

"Exactly. That's when you'll be in grave danger. Do you have a weapon?"

"No."

"Do you prefer an Army Colt of a Glock 9mm?"

"The Glock."

"That is the best choice." The Colonel took up the pistol and a box of cartridges from the seat beside him and handed it to Dan.

"You were pretty sure I'd take the job." The colonel with his strange powers had read Dan correctly, in that he would take the job. Had he also determined the real reason Dan had taken the job?

"I wasn't totally sure, but had a good guess. And so I wanted to have what you would need. Do you have a car?"

"Yeah. It's got some years on it but I've worked on the engine and it'll roll with the best of them."

"Good." The Colonel took an envelope from an inside pocket and handed it to Dan. "Here's $5,000 for starters. I'll set up an account with my lawyer and get the information as to who he is to you. Also inside is the addresses of the places you will find me most of the time. I have a home on the lake north of town. And an apartment and office downtown. I've jotted my phone numbers down."

"How much time do I have to pull this off?"

"I've no idea. The man will have seen the sergeant with me and will know I'm being careful. Now once he sees you stalking me, that'll further slow him down for he'll want to find out who you are. Even kill you. Keep your job at the club. I don't want him to know that I've hired you. Follow me when you're off duty, or get somebody to work your shift so that you have free time."

Dan nodded, digesting what had been told to him. He had drawn an assassin's bullet from the colonel to himself.

"Please hear me plain. This man is very dangerous. He's a huge man, much bigger than you."

"I've fought big men before."

"Not like this one. Don't fight him. All I want you to do is to tell me where to find him. Use the pistol only for self defense."

"And once you know, you'll take it from there," Dan said.

The colonel aimed his crystal crusted eyes at Dan and didn't say a word. The colonel had seen combat up close and would know what to do with an enemy.

"Suppose I can't find out who this fellow is?"

"I'm certain you'll give it your best effort. One last thing, if you need help such as running a license plate number, call Ethan. He has a Marine buddy in the police department."

Ethan nodded. "His name is Alan Hickman, a lieutenant of detectives in homicide. Here's my phone number. Call me when you need something that he can help you with, or that I can do for you." He handed Dan a slip of paper.

The colonel spoke to the sergeant. "Sergeant, we have done good work here tonight. So back to the club."

"Yes, sir."

Chapter Six

Under the burning Baghdad sun, Kristin crouched behind the mud wall surrounding one of the small block houses lining the narrow street. The other members of her squad of Marines were scattered both left and right of her, some behind the wall with her, others inside the nearer houses. The insurgents, from the windows and rooftops of close by buildings, poured an intense rifle fire upon the outnumbered Marines. The storm of bullets knocked chunks out of the wall and the block buildings. Marines popped up from behind the wall or from the windows of the houses to shoot back and immediately duck back down for safety.

Kristin rose from behind the wall to aim her rifle at a man firing from an open window on the ground floor of one of the houses. Her weapon was on full automatic and she held the trigger down and fired a stream of bullets. The recoil of the weapon jarred her. The familiar kick of the weapon was a satisfying thing. They were under heavy attack, and it was good to kill the enemy before they killed her, or one of her comrades.

She saw her bullets pour into the open window and slam the man firing from it back into the room and down out of sight. At that moment a woman dragging a little girl by the hand darted out of a building and into view. With legs kicking the tails of their matching yellow dresses, they ran directly into Kristin's rain of bullets. They were cut down, knees folding, arms flying. They fell slack and lifeless, rolling in the dust of the street.

Kristin stopped firing and raised her rifle to point at the sky. Oblivious to the bullets exploding pieces from the wall and stinging her with the shards, she stared at the crumpled bodies of the woman and girl lying on the street. Her eyes became fixed on the blood gushing from the horrible wounds and rapidly staining the thin cotton dresses with crimson and forming puddles in the dust of the street.

"My God. My God. What have I done?" Kristin moaned in her sleep. She abruptly jerked awake and sat up in the bed. She hastily flung a look around in the half darkness surrounding her. She recognized the furnishings of her apartment.

"Not again," she moaned. "My God, not again."

She grabbed her head in both hands and squeezed with all her strength. Stop the nightmare, squeeze all those damnable memories out, make them stop coming so painfully, haunting her, destroying her.

After a time, the length of which Kristin did not know, she released her head. Moving slowly, shakily she climbed out of bed and sat on the edge of it with her feet on the floor.

"Damnation," she said. She rose and crossed to the bathroom and turned on the cold water faucet and washed her face with big double handfuls. She lifted her head and looked at her dripping face in the mirror.

"Murderer. You're a damned murderer." She turned away shuddering at the sight of her face.

* * * * *

Dan, resting in a much worn easy chair with his feet cocked up on a stool, was deeply immersed in a thick book. A bag of pretzels and a bottle of beer were on a small table at his elbow. The apartment was a cheap one on the first floor of an old three story house in the poorer part of Chicago. It was a two room affair, just a front room and kitchen combination and a bedroom with the door standing open. It was messy like most bachelors' dens.

He was deep into the chapter that described the neural pathways of the brain, at least those so far discovered, and did not hear the first rapping of knuckles on his door. The second knocking was louder, more insistent. Who could it be so late in the night? He dropped the book on the chair, crossed the room and opened the door.

Dan was surprised to see Kristin Goodfolk standing in the doorway. He thought her expression showed uncertainty at being here, even bashfulness. She had discarded her slacks and Marine jacket, now wearing a stylish maroon coat over a lighter shade maroon dress. The heels on her shoes made her as tall as Dan and appear more slender then he remembered. Her hair was neatly done, and makeup made her face appeared less drawn, less troubled. She was quite pretty being dressed as a woman should be, Dan thought.

"Hello, hero." Kristin said and held up a bottle of wine and a bag containing something. "Would you care to share some Italian carryout and a bottle of wine?"

"Hello, Kristin," Dan said and gave her a big smile. "Sure sounds better than pretzels and beer."

"Then let's dine on the bounty that I've brought." Kristin said, pleased at Dan's friendly greeting.

Dan made a sweeping motion inviting Kristin to enter. "Do come in Bearer Of Good Food."

Feeling glad for Kristin's company, Dan helped her remove her coat. Then he hurried about setting the table. Kristin removed the contents from the paper bag and placed them on the table. As of one accord, they sat down across from each other.

"We work good together," Kristin said and looking into Dan's eyes.

"That we do."

"Then I'm not a bother."

"Far from that. I must admit something. I have been thinking about you ever since we met yesterday. So thanks for coming to visit."

Kristin nodded at the food. "Then let's eat while everything is still warm."

Kristin and Dan heaped their plates with food, filled their glasses with dark red wine and dined at the small kitchen table. They often smiled at ease and enjoying each other's company.

Kristin spoke. "You don't remember me from before the colonel's dream session? Do you?"

"Had I seen you before that?"

"I'm in your Ethics class at the university. Yeah, I know there's at least a hundred students in that class. And more than half are girls. So I understand why you've never noticed me."

"I should have. Next time I'll look for you. What's you major?"

"Geology."

"That's a man's game. There's a lot of traveling and rugged field work."

"It's not just a man's game anymore. There are many women in the field. And besides, I want to know all I can about this big ball of rock and water that we live on."

"I would too. But that'll have to come later after I get my doctorate."

"What's your major?"

"Neuroscience. I want to know how and why the brains thinks in the way it does."

Kristin's face took on a somber expression. "I'd like to know the same thing. Do you want to know why I came here tonight?"

"It's because I'm so damn handsome that you couldn't resist me."

Kristin gave Dan a small smile. "Not really. Well, maybe a little. It's because you've been over there in the fighting and know what it's like. Probably seen and done the same things that I have."

"Most likely."

"Killed people?"

"Yeah."

Kristin's eyes fill with tears. "I can live with killing men who're trying to kill me. But I've killed innocent people."

"Other Marines have too."

"Not like I did. And it's tearing me apart. My squad was on patrol when we came under fire from some of those walled houses they have. I was returning fire at the man in the bottom floor. On full automatic and really pouring it on. Then this woman dragging a little girl by the hand runs right into my fire." Kristin shuddered. "I chopped her and the little girl into pieces. I can still see the bullets ripping them apart. The little girl's head was blown off her body. It just exploded."

Kristin began to sob, the tears pouring in rivulets down her cheeks. "Dan, I killed two innocent people. Every night, I have nightmares of shooting that woman and little girl. I shoot them over and over and see them flying into pieces."

Dan quickly rose and knelt beside Kristin's chair. He took her into his arms and hugged her tightly to him. He whispered to her, "You're not alone in shooting the wrong people. I know several men who killed innocent bystanders."

"Did you ever?"

"No. But it was just dumb luck that kept me from doing it. We were on patrol and passing this group of young men standing beside the road. I was watching them close for I was sure most of them would have guns hidden in their clothing. This one fellow, just a big kid, stuck his hand inside his jacket. I thought he was reaching for a gun. So I put mine on him and was ready to shoot when he brings out a pack of smokes. I sure could've shot an innocent that time."

Dan watched Kristin as she wiped tears away with her napkin. She gave him a bright smile.

"I'm all right now. It all just gets to me sometimes."

"You sure you're okay? Anything I can do for you?"

"I'm all right now. I shouldn't have let go like that."

"Why not? You're with a friend who understands. Who damn well understands."

"Thanks for that," Kristin said and brightened. "Guess I just needed a little conversation and sympathy. It's getting late now, I'd better go and let you get some sleep."

Dan released Kristin, stood and checked his watch. "It sure is late. And much too late for you to be out on the street in this neighborhood. And besides, I have a favor to ask."

"I owe you so what's the favor?"

"Would you stay over and be sure to wake me up so that I can get to class on time?"

"What? Wake you?" Kristin acted surprised. She really wasn't, this was what she had wanted once she had quieted after the dream in her apartment. To be held by this fellow who had helped her at the dream session.

Dan nodded. "If you have bad dreams, then I can talk with you and that'll make it easier. In the morning, we can have breakfast and go to school together. How does that strike you?

"Well, we could do that." Kristin's eyes were locked on Dan's.

"There's one problem with that plan."

"What's that?"

"I only have one bed."

"Well, if you have only one bed, we'd better set the alarm for we'll be mighty tired by morning," Kristin replied and broke into a soft laugh.

Dan stepped close to Kristin and scooped her up in his arms. The good feel of her against him made him chuckle.

"What's funny?" she asked and pressed her face against his chest.

"I was remembering what a friend said about a pretty woman."

"What was that?"

"They are the very best tonic for what ails a man."

"Is that a compliment?"

"The very highest."

"Then I accept it."

A thought came to Dan as he carried Kristin toward the bedroom. Had Colonel Granville, the Master Dreamer, somehow played a hand in Kristin showing up at Dan's apartment? Ethan had said the colonel added some ingredient to the dreams to help the troubled veterans heal from the damage being done by memories of fighting and killing. Dan was angered at the possibility that the colonel might have intruded into his life so deeply. Yet at the same time, he was glad for Kristin's presence in his world.

Chapter Seven

Dan drew on a heavy coat and cap, locked his apartment behind him, and left the house by the rear door. He crossed the yard to a black 1972 Chevelle Super Sport parked on a concrete slab abutting the alley. He ran his hand over the shiny hood of the car. He had put a lot of work into the SS and was very fond of it.

The SS had been in the family from the time it was mint new. Shortly after the death of Dan's grandmother, his grandfather had bought the car. Some members of the family had said the old man had acquired the muscle car, the SS was built for racing, so that he could lavish on it the attention he had lavished on the wife that he so dearly loved. The old man did take great care of the vehicle. Dan had often helped his grandfather wash, wax and lubricate it. He would nod in agreement with the old man when he bragged about the power and stream-lined beauty of the vehicle. Dan learned to drive sitting behind its steering wheel. When his grandfather had grown frail and could no longer drive, he had parked the car in the garage and locked the door on it. His grandfather had died while Dan was fighting in Afghanistan. He had left the car to Dan. Upon returning to civilian life, Dan spent more than a year overhauling the vehicle, now more than thirty years old, taking it apart piece by piece for a full inspection, replacing old and worn parts, disassembling the engine entirely and cleaning and honing everything. Lastly he reinstalled all the chrome on the outside and that on the engine under the hood. The SS was in as good a condition as when it was new. Ethan had his two tonics for recovery from fighting and killing, the beautiful girl and Master Dreamer. Dan had his SS as a tonic.

He climbed into the car and drove down the alley and turned left onto a street heading north. He silently repeated the address of his destination and then bent to his driving.

Nearly a score of miles later, Dan had left the city behind and was cruising the SS along a narrow black-top road lined with thick woods. He glanced at the numbers on the mailboxes at the beginning of the narrow lanes spaced every hundred yards or so and leading off into the woods. The lanes were visible but a short distance up their lengths before vanishing into the darkness.

Spotting the number he wanted, he continued on past for a few car lengths where he pulled onto the side of the road and stopped. He sat quietly and watched the empty road, the dark woods and the nearby lanes. Seeing nothing that might mean danger, he got out of the SS and quickly locked the car. He drew his pistol, pulled his coat tightly about him and stole into the woods.

Dan moved silently with the light from a half moon but a frail thing, mostly blocked by the limbs of the trees overhead. Still the light was sufficient for him to see where he stepped and to dodge under the low hanging tree branches. He felt the wash of caution and tenseness of a Marine going into hostile territory settle over him.

He came upon the shore of Lake Michigan and heard the wet sounds of the waves striking and dying upon the stony shore. Two ducks on the water, frightened by his appearance, took to the air with a noisy flap of wings, and disappeared into the night lying black on the lake.

Dan veered off along the waterline, circling around the huge boulders that had been dropped twelve millennia ago by the great glacier that had covered Michigan. He had gone but a short distance when he halted and peered ahead through the trees. A large, two-story house with a long porch with pillars sat in a clearing in the woods and facing the lake. The house glowed eerily in the moonbeams slanting in from the east. Muted light shone in four windows on the ground floor. A lawn extended down to the lake shore where there was a boat dock with a motor boat tied up to it. This was Colonel Granville's lake house.

Dan slipped ahead to a big stand of evergreen shrubbery bordering the lawn. Tense, wary, he examined the house. Questions raced through his mind. Was the colonel home? Was the stalker here same as Dan? The stalker must see Dan watching the colonel for the plan to work. The lake house would be the most suitable place for the stalker to attack the colonel. Had Dan made the trip here for nothing?

He heard a ragged cough in the shrubbery on his right. He spun and pointed the pistol in the direction of the sound.

"Come out of their before I put half a dozen rounds into you," Dan commanded.

Nothing stirred. The seconds drag past.

"Come out, damn you," Dan ordered harshly. "I'll not tell you again."

"Don't shoot. I'm coming." The words came in an old man's raspy voice.

The shrubbery parted and a stooped figure with a tattered blanket wrapped about it shuffled into view.

"Hold up, fellow. Don't shoot me."

Dan eyed the man, taking in his blanket and worn clothing. A street person. Or more accurately, a bush person.

"What the hell you doing there?"

"Just trying to get through the night. It's mighty cold."

"Don't you have a place to get inside?"

"I've got a little tent back in there. But the night's early and I've got no heat."

"Talk sense," Dan said angrily, still tense from the discovery of the man. "You're out here in the woods wrapped in a blanket. Now you tell me that because the night's early, you've got no heat. What the hell has early got to do with it?"

The man shrank back at Dan's harsh words and said nothing.

"Damnit. Talk to me."

The man straightened as much as his old body could and faced Dan squarely. He pointed at the house.

"The man who lives there is still up. When he goes to bed, I stretch out my cable and plug my little electric heater into his outside outlet and keep warm in my tent."

The words got to Dan. "You a vet?" he asked in a kinder tone.

"Yep. Four years in Viet Nam with the Marines. Did some tough fighting too. Helped my buddies take some stupid hills from the little brown men that we turned around and gave back to them. You ever hear of Hill 875 near Dak To in Vietnam?"

"No."

The man eyed Dan through the weak moonlight. "What we did there was in all the American papers at the time. But I reckon you wouldn't know anything about it for I'm talking about back in the late 1968 and that'd be years before you were in God's world. That was a stupid war fighting for stupid hills. You know what the military geniuses say, take the high ground. Well we took a lot of high ground and still lost the war."

The old man moved a few halting steps closer to Dan and stared levelly at him.

"Now you see me here without a pot to piss in. Sure, I take a little electricity, but just a few pennies a night. Look at that big house. Any man who can own that wouldn't ever miss it. And I don't mean any harm to any man who walks the earth."

Dan studied the old man so forlorn in the cold night. He wondered how many other vets were sleeping in the bushes of some other man's house.

"You're not going to arrest me, are you?" the old man questioned anxiously.

"No. A man has to live as best he can."

"That sure as hell sounds good to me. I don't think that other fella would'a seen it that way."

Dan was instantly alert. "What other fellow?"

"The one that stood over there in the edge of the yard about a quarter hour ago. He was watching the house just like you did."

Dan quickly swept the woods all around. Someone could have slipped up on him while he and the old vet were talking.

"He's not here now," said the man, seeing Dan sudden reaction. "Went and looked in the windows and then went down by the lake and checked the boat. After that I lost sight of him."

"What'd he look like?"

"Big sonofabitch. Sure bigger than you. Even big like that, he just floated over the ground without a sound. Quiet as death itself. I had this feeling he'd kill me if he found me. So I played the rabbit and stayed in my foxhole."

Dan evaluated what he had been told. Then he spoke to the man. "What's your name?"

"Frank Tanner."

Dan dug out his wallet and handed the man several bills. "Here, Frank, take this. I want you to watch for the other man and tell me what he does the next time I come here."

"So you're coming back," said the man as he held the bills up and tried to read the denominations. "Can't see what they are since my eyes ain't what they used to be and the moon is weak. But thank you just the same."

"They're twenties. I came into an inheritance a couple of days ago."

"I could sure as hell use an inheritance. I'll watch for the big bastard. But I'm not going to let him see me doing it. You be careful too. He could be close and listening to us at this very time."

"I'll keep an eye peeled. Go back to your tent."

"You must have been a Marine once too to be so kind to me." The man turned and shuffled back into the bushes.

Dan stared after the old Marine. Be safe, he silently whispered, for he had given the man a dangerous assignment.

Dan stole across the yard and looked into one of the windows that showed light behind a drawn blind. He could see nothing around the edges of the tightly fitting blind. He moved to the next window, and the last two and all were masked by drawn blinds. The colonel wasn't going to make himself an easy target, if he was indeed here in the house.

The moon hid behind a cloud as Dan made his way down to the dock to look at the boat. He found the craft to be a 16 foot outboard. Nothing further could be learned here. He trotted across the yard to the woods and entered the darkness under the tall trees. He oriented himself, and mostly feeling his way among the big tree trunks, set a course toward the SS.

He halted a few steps back from the edge of the woods and peered intently ahead. Through an opening in the woods, the faint outline of the SS could just barely be made out setting on the side of the road. He felt reluctant to leave the protection of the woods and go to the car. The old man had seen the stalker. That man could have found the SS and now be hiding in ambush nearby and waiting for Dan to offer himself as a target.

Dan let the seconds drag past. Nothing moved. No sound reached him. A minute passed. Two more. Three more. Better to be patient than to be dead.

Finally Dan moved to stand pressed against the trunk of a large tree at the edge of the woods. He keenly examined the SS and the area around it. Nothing.

The crunch of a leaf, the slightest of sound, stirred the air in Dan's ear. He hurled himself to the ground on his stomach. He flung a look in the direction of the sound, just as two pistol shots blasted streaks of reddish-orange fire from the darkness of the woods.

The bullets hammered the tree where he had leaned but a moment before. Splinters of wood exploded and flew. That could have been Dan's skull exploding.

Dan swung his pistol and fired three fast rounds. One directly at the location of the shots, then one just to the left and one to the right of the location of his attacker's shots. He rolled to get away from the pistol flashes that marked his position. He lay motionlessly, his heart pounding. His eyes searched the black woods, the pistol ready.

The darkness lay silent. He caught no movement. Nothing to tell where his attacker was now. Or if he had been hit by Dan's bullets.

Dan now knew his attacker was a most patient man. Dan would prove he was the more patient of the two. Let his enemy make the first move.

Dan cocked his ears and concentrated on all the small noises of the woods, searching for the one that was not natural, that should not be there. There had been other times when he had waited for the enemy to move and give himself away. The moon sailed out from behind the cloud and brought its light to the woods. Dan rolled his head and minutely examined the SS and all around it.

The minutes dragged past. Dan did not stir. The moon hid itself behind a small cloud. Dan could use the darkness to steal away into the woods. But, damn it, he wasn't going to leave the SS to the stalker. The man would recognize the uniqueness of the SS and its great value to Dan. He would steal it or destroy it out of anger at Dan's escape.

Dan measured the moon and the cloud behind which it hid. He had maybe a minute to act. Maybe half a minute with the moon light blocked out. With the warrior's sense for daring, of being up to doing battle, Dan leapt to his feet and sprinted to the SS. He jumped into the driver's seat and keyed the ignition. The engine rumbled to life. When he lifted his head to drive away, he saw a square of paper stuck under the wiper blade, partially obscuring his vision straight ahead.

He immediately knew the paper had been placed there by the stalker, and most likely had been done to slow Dan's leaving. He would not play that game. He peered around the paper, gunned the powerful engine of the SS, and hurtled away.

Dan glanced at the rear view mirror and checked behind. Just as the moon broke free of the cloud and its rays fell upon a man racing into the roadway, to stop and stare after him. I made it, you bastard, Dan whispered. Still he was impressed by the man's quickness to adapt to Dan's appearance at the colonel's house, and his recognition of how the SS could be used as bait to lure Dan into a trap.

Dan laughed with relief at his escape, and the new knowledge he had learned. The colonel was correct, there was a stalker, and a deadly one. Dan had accomplished the first part of his task. The stalker now knew of Dan. The second part, to learn the man's identity without getting killed, was going to be much more difficult.

* * * * *

Dan slowed and pulled into a gravel lane and stopped out of sight of anyone passing on the road. He rolled down the window and reached out and removed the paper from under the windshield wiper. Under the dome light, he read the words written in bold capital letters on the paper. WHAT KIND OF DREAMS DO YOU DREAM???

Dan frowned as he folded the note and shoved it into a shirt pocket. What the hell kind of a question was that? Especially from a man who had tried to kill him. He snapped off the light and sat staring out into the night. The colonel could bring dreams to many men, and all at the same time. Ethan believed those dreams could be used to heal the heads of battle damaged veterans. Now this stalker asked about dreams.

Dan closed his eyes and leaned his head back against the seat. He listened to the pleasant rumble of the engine of the SS. Normally it was a soothing sound. Tonight it failed in its task for Dan could not prevent the events of the past two days from racing through his mind. What was the connection between the stalker and the colonel and all this discussion about dreams? Two things were damn clear, he had gotten himself into a situation of danger, and most strangely, that danger seemed to be centered on dreams.

Dan pulled out his cell phone and dialed. Spoke a few words and snapped it closed.

He shifted into gear and rolled the SS slowly and without lights to the foot of the lane. There he stopped and checked the road both ways. It lay empty. He snapped on the headlights, gunned the engine and burst out of the lane and off along the road.

Dream Hitcher

* * * * *

Dan entered the small bar called Pookey's Place, a horrible name, but served unique and quite delightful private brand beer. He spotted Ethan, who had agreed to meet with him, seated at a table and he crossed to him and sat down.

"Hello, Ethan," Dan said in greeting.

"Hello yourself. What're you drinking?"

"Same as you."

Ethan held up his mug to the bartender and motioned at Dan. The bartender nodded.

The two men sat silently until the beer had been delivered and the bartender had retreated behind the bar.

Dan took a deep swig of the beer. "Good," he said. "I needed a lift."

He removed the note, now in an envelope, from his shirt pocket.

"There's a note in this to me. It was on the windshield of my car when I got done spying on the colonel's house. I found it there after our mystery man tried to shoot me."

"You hurt?" Ethan asked quickly.

"Nope, he missed. But close."

"Then you actually saw him?"

"I didn't see him for it was too dark for that. He was waiting for me when I got back to my car."

"How did you get away?"

"Pulled my pistol and fired a few rounds. Don't know if I hit him. Probably not for he's damn good in the woods. The colonel's gun came in handy."

"Too bad that you couldn't have ended it there. What does the note say?

"Just a few words and all in caps. WHAT KIND OF DREAMS DO YOU DREAM??? With three question marks at the end. That's all he wrote. It must be like the colonel said. The man likes to play games with people. But this time he's left something behind that proves he's real. Do you want to read it?"

"No. Knowing what it said is enough. Better not get anymore fingerprints on it and confuse the police."

Dan handed the envelope to Ethan. "Have your friend Hickman check it for fingerprints. Some of mine are on it. He can separate them from any others."

"Do you think this fellow would be dumb enough to leave prints?"

"No. Unless he's cock-sure that nobody will ever catch him. Or he knows there's no record of his prints anyplace."

"You'd better watch your ass. This fellow might get lucky the next time."

"While he was leaving the note, he surely took down my license plate number. Now he can easily find out who I am and where I live."

"I wouldn't want him breathing down my neck. I think you should come with me to see Hickman. He'll want to talk with you personally about how you came by this note."

"All right. Set it up. I'll call the colonel and report what happened."

Chapter Eight

Anubis cruised the Porsche along the Chicago night street. He was keyed up and watching the streets. He saw the usual late night street scene with the whores on their corners and waving and showing their mostly naked bodies to get the Johns to stop. The street people were wandering about, or sitting drunk or sleeping on the sidewalk. Groups of young men, some black, some brown, some white were standing on their piece of turf, ready to defend it against invaders. Innocent common folk hurried along on private errands and hoping all the time not to get mugged.

Anubis had no interest in these people. He was looking for something unique. He sped up with the cross streets flashing past. The HUNT was on.

He wheeled the Porsche onto a street lined on both sides with tall office buildings. He slowed and leaned forward to look up through the top part of the windshield at the soaring office buildings reaching for the sky. The half open eye of the moon darted in and out between the buildings as the Porsche rolled onward.

The steel skeleton of a multi-story building under construction came into view further ahead. The top of the 57-floor structure would have been lost in the sky, had it not been for the flaming arcs of half a score of welding torches of steel workers, and a flood light illuminating their work area. Sparks of molten steel sprayed out crimson, orange and yellow from the welding torches. The sparkling light from the falling shower of sparks died to black at about the fiftieth floor.

Anubis continued closer and lowered his vision to the steel workers vehicles, mostly pickups, pulled up close to the base of the building. On the street close by the pickups, a sedan drove up and three black men climbed out and looked up at the welders. They leaned against the sedan. Waiting.

Anubis pulled the Porsche to the curb half a block from the black men and stopped. He got out of the car and stood looking up at the workers.

As he watched, the welding torches went black. The last falling spark of molten metal blinked out. The floodlight flicked off. Shortly a yellow light began to descend the side of the structure. He knew this was a light in the cage elevator, fastened to the outside of the structure, which was carrying the workers to the ground.

He saw the black men move to the far side of their car and out of sight of anyone on the elevator. They peered over the car at the elevator.

The elevator reached the ground and the workmen, all Zuni Indians, climbed out. They stood for half a minute in the light of the elevator and talking, then separated and moved off toward their parked vehicles.

Anubis came to attention when one of the black men came out from behind the sedan and fell in behind a Zuni heading for his pickup.

"Hey, Indian, wait up a minute," the black man called.

The Zuni stopped and turned. He looked at the man and then at the sedan. He half turned and looked at the other Zunis, who where climbing into their vehicles. He seemed on the verge of calling out to them. Then, as he hesitated, it was too late for they were driving away.

He turned back to the black man who had come up close. He glanced past the man to the other two men who had come out from behind the car and was hurrying toward them.

Anubis watching the four men, heard angry voices erupt. In the dull light from the elevator, he saw the black men jump the Zuni.

The Zuni struck out hard and fast in defense. One of the men staggered back. Then the other two pounce upon the Zuni, striking him fiercely. They captured his arms and held him while the third man began to punch him, concentrating on his ribs and stomach.

Anubis heard the sodden thuds of the blows striking the Zuni's body. He dashed toward the fight, more a beating.

"Hold up there!" Anubis shouted out ahead.

The black men snapped alert, pivoted and focused on Anubis advancing upon them. They swept him with hard eyes, measuring him for size and how much trouble he brought. The black man that had done the hitting took a threatening step toward Anubis.

"What the fuck do you want?"

"I want to talk with the Indian. So leave him able to do that."

"He owes me money. He fucks my ladies and won't pay them. He'll sure come up with the money after this lesson. Now get the hell out of here before we give you some of the same." He raised his fist to show Anubis the brass knuckles he wore. They caught the light and gleamed.

Anubis laughed mockingly; this was better than he had hoped. He stepped closer to the black, who swung his brass knuckled fist at Anubis' face.

Anubis' hand flashed out and captured the fist in mid strike. He twisted it and bones broke with sharp crackling sounds. A high pitch screech of pain erupted from the injured man.

Anubis jerked the man up close, slammed him under the chin with the heel of his hand which snapped his head back at an unnatural angle, and broke his neck. Anubis flung the man aside and moved upon the remaining two blacks.

They released the Zuni to collapse on the ground. One raised his fists and jumped to meet Anubis. The second jammed a hand into a coat pocket.

Anubis swung a big fist at the black coming at him and connected with a crushing blow, knocking him aside and down onto the ground.

Immediately he leapt at the third black pulling a pistol from his pocket. He caught the hand and pistol and held it for a moment. Then he laughed and began to slowly force the pistol up. The man struggled mightily to halt the rise. He couldn't against Anubis' strength. The pistol stopped with it thrust up under the man's chin.

Anubis looked into the man's frightened eyes and spoke calmly. "Now fire away whenever you're ready."

At that suggestion, the black man's eyes filled with terror. He vigorously shook his head. He sure as hell wasn't going to pull the trigger.

"Oh, come on," Anubis said in a pleasant voice. "Put three ounces of pressure on the trigger and make it go bang."

The man shook his head. "Let me go, mister. Please let me go."

"I'll do that just a soon as you make the gun go bang."

The man shook his head, as much as he could with the barrel of the pistol buried deeply under his chin.

"Then let me help you." Anubis put a finger on top of the man's that was on the trigger and began to press down, all the time looking into the man's eyes.

The gun fired. Gray brain matter and fragments of skull bone explode from the top of the man's head. Anubis took the gun from the man's hand and flung the limp body away.

He stepped to the two unconscious men on the ground, and aimed the pistol down at the forehead of one. He hesitated for a moment, then shrugged and shot the man. He stepped to the second man and shot him in a similar place.

He pocketed the pistol and sighed with regret. "What a damn waste of beautiful dreams" he said to the night.

He turned to the Zuni sagging against the side of his pickup. "How bad are you hurt?"

The Zuni wiped blood from his lips with the back of his hand and spit a mouthful of blood onto the ground.

"Got some busted ribs and that's for sure. But I believe I'll live."

"That's good. And there's another good thing about all of all this. You won't have to worry about paying your debts to these fellows."

The Zuni studied Anubis closely. "Why'd you helped me?"

"Zuni's are famous for their fearless work on the high steel of tall buildings. I know that bands of you go all over the world doing your trade. A man with bravery like that would make for interesting conversation. Now let's get you fixed up. My car is just over there. Can you walk?"

"Yeah. Sure. I've been hurt worse than this. Slipped once and fell to the end of my safety harness. Would've fell sixty floors without it. Broke some ribs and fractured my spine that time."

"Seems like you're a tough one. But even so it's best we get you to a doctor right away. Come get in my car."

Holding his side and moving gingerly, the Zuni walked beside Anubis to the Porsche, and climbed into the passenger seat.

Anubis got in behind the wheel. He looked at the Zuni holding his ribs and grimacing with pain.

"Those ribs seem to be hurting you."

"The broke ends are jabbing me something fierce."

"There's a needle there in the glove box. It has something in it that'll make you feel better until we get you to a doctor."

"What's in it?"

"A mixture that I've used before. Good stuff. You'll like it."

"I'll give it a try."

He opened the glove box and took out a capped syringe.

"It's powerful stuff, so just use half of it," Anubis warned.

The Zuni injected a portion of the contents into his arm and returned the syringe to the glove box. He relaxed back into the seat.

* * * * *

Anubis slowed at the entrance to the cemetery and swept a close look out over the sprawling area of rocks standing on end. He proceeded slowly up the paved winding driveway among the tombstones to the far side of the cemetery. He stopped below a small rise that hid the Porsche from the road.

He looked down at the Zuni lying slack, his muscles frozen by Anubis' concoction of drugs. The Zuni's eyes burn with rage for he knew he had been tricked into taking the drug.

"I lied to you," Anubis said. "That needle didn't hold what you expected."

The Zuni struggled to break free of the paralysis caused by the drug. His work hardened body quivered with the mighty effort.

"Relax," said Anubis. "It's your destiny to be here with me at this precise moment in time. And I promise you that this won't be as bad as you think."

Anubis searched the Zuni's pockets and removed his wallet from a rear pocket. He opened it and checked for identification.

"Walking Buffalo Yazzie is a good name for someone going on a long journey."

Anubis reached across the Zuni and took the syringe from the glove box. He looked into Walking Buffalo's eyes. There was no fear there. Only burning rage and hate. Anubis smiled, delighted at the Zuni's expression.

"You're a brave man and I'm glad that you are, for brave men have the most fascinating of all journeys into the next world. I feel most privileged to join you in that journey."

He pulled the cap off the syringe. "It's time for our journey. Yes, ours for I plan to join you. I must hear the music and feel the wind of the afterlife blow cross my face. And see where your journey ends."

Anubis injected the remainder of the drug mixture into Walking Buffalo's thigh. Then with high anticipation, he leaned and put his head against that of Walking Buffalo's.

Anubis easily connected with Walking Buffalo's thoughts and the humming sound like that of a hive of bees, instantly followed by a kaleidoscope of colorful and swiftly shifting pattern of pictures that abruptly settled into a live scene. The bee hum ceased.

Anubis found himself on a broad, flat valley blanketed with new grass of a green ever so lovely color appearing soft as satin. Tall sandstone mesas, gleaming golden in the pure sunlight, surrounded the valley on three sides. A band of sheep white as new snow grazed on the far side of a meandering stream. One giant cottonwood grew beside the steam. The land was a grand vista to behold.

Walking Buffalo, hale and hardy, stood and drank in the magnificent scene. This was his land, and he was at peace.

Anubis, standing three steps behind the Zuni, frowned, disturbed. He cocked his ear and turned his head straining to hear. Strangely there was total silence. No celestial orchestra played here.

Walking Buffalo moved off swiftly toward the stream. Anubis, still troubled, followed three steps behind.

From out of nowhere, a coyote appeared under the big cottonwood. The coyote was playing with a blue butterfly, jumping and making mock strikes at the little aviator that flitted about with a flutter of translucent wings. Both the coyote and the butterfly were greatly enjoying the friendly game.

Walking Buffalo and Anubis drew close to the game players and halted. As they stared at the coyote, it began to change, the head, legs metamorphosing. In a second the coyote had become an old, gray headed Zuni, dressed in immaculately clean tanned deer hide jumper, pants and moccasins. His gray hair was tied in a long queue that hung down past his shoulders.

Anubis threw a quick look at Walking Buffalo and saw him smile knowingly at the transformation. He had seen this happen before.

The old man lifted a wooden flute to his lips and began to blow and a lovely tune came forth. The blue butterfly began an aerial dance to the music, turning and wheeling in graceful looping patterns in front of the old man.

The old man started to dance to his own music, spinning and bowing and all the while watching the butterfly as he played. The butterfly fell into rhythm with the man. It pirouetted on the point of one gossamer wing and then the other, followed by a series of small vertical loops.

The old man began to spin. The butterfly held fixed station in front of him and spun with him as if the two were fastened together. The man's face showed pleasure, and the movements of the butterfly told that it also was having a fine time.

The man pretended to catch sight of Walking Buffalo for the first time. He halted his dance and removed the flute from his lips. His aged, wrinkled face became wreathed in a mischievous expression.

The butterfly ceased its dance and hovered in front of the man as if asking why he had stopped the music. The man ignored the butterfly. After a moment of waiting, the tiny aviator, performed an upside down loop, caught an elevator of wind and vanished into the sky.

With the disappearance of the butterfly, the music of the universe came alive, a celestial orchestra of string instruments, winds, percussions, and other instruments never before heard by living humans. The volume started low and steadily rose, becoming ever more beautiful.

"Hello, Coyote Man," Walking Buffalo said. "I see you're still up to your tricks."

Coyote Man smiled, his old cheeks crinkling into a hundred folds of pleasure.

"Hello, Walking Buffalo, my friend."

"Your flute playing was beautiful as always."

"Thank you. But the music came from the flute. I was merely setting it free."

"That's what you told me when I was a boy."

"You've been gone a very long time. Still, I waited for I knew you would return one day. All of our people do no matter how far away they've traveled."

"It's good to be home."

Walking Buffalo looked about in all directions. "I would like to ride one of my cayuses, but I don't see them. Do you know where they are?"

"The whirlwind knows where you can find your golden horses. Follow it and it will lead you there." Coyote Man lifted his flute and pointed with it.

Walking Buffalo turned to look in the direction indicted. Anubis turned to look also.

In the valley but a short distance away there was a whirlwind, a vortex thirty feet tall of shining silver grains. It spun gently with the slightest of undulations along its length. A pleasant wind sound came from it and added one more instrument to the celestial orchestra.

Walking Buffalo took the presence of the whirlwind as nothing unusual.

Anubis stood transfixed and watched the whirling silver particles.

Walking Buffalo spoke to Coyote Man. "I'll say goodbye for now."

"Goodbye, Walking Buffalo."

Walking Buffalo moved toward the whirlwind. Immediately the whirling silver plume glided off along the stream. Walking Buffalo broke into a happy, bounding run after the whirlwind and matching its speed.

Anubis ran directly behind Walking Buffalo. His step was effortless as if there were no gravity. He had decided to go with the Zuni to the end of his journey. If he did not like the final destination, he could always return to the land of the living. He was certain of that, even if he hadn't yet made such a trip.

The whirlwind skimmed over the creek. The men followed behind, their feet splashing the water with a musical sound. The moment they come out of the creek, four long legged, palomino horses were in sight grazing the grass not far off.

The whirlwind halted its forward movement, spun for a second and stopped. Its silver grains hung twinkling throughout its form. Then leisurely, like feathers floating downward, the whirlwind collapsed. The silver grains stopped falling just above the ground and spread out into a layer of silver ground fog.

Walking Buffalo cried out a shrill, happy voice. "AIII!"

The palominos lifted their heads. One snorted and neighed in greeting to Walking Buffalo. Then as of one accord, they all raced to meet him.

Walking Buffalo ran into the fog and it parted for his feet and rippled around his legs to his knees. With each step, a lovely musical chord came alive and blended with his happy laughter. He broke from the fog and raced onward.

Anubis followed after Walking Buffalo. His feet struck the silver fog and it was like wet concrete and he started to fall. He caught his balance at the last moment. He looked down at the fog sticking to his feet and clinging to his legs up to the knees. He stepped forward and more of the silver fog collected onto his legs. He plowed on, laboriously, a short step at a time.

After hardly a body length, he was brought to a halt by the large silver mass gripping his legs. He looked for Walking Buffalo.

The Zuni had reached the golden horses and was moving among them and stroking their beautiful heads and arched necks. The horses nickered and snorted and toss their heads with gladness at seeing the man.

Walking Buffalo sprang upon the back of the most grand of the horses. Sitting proudly erect, he rode off at a gallop, with the remaining three horses bounding along beside him.

Anubis took a step backward and part of the heavy silver fog fell from his legs. Another step backward and more fog dropped away. He continued his back stepping and pulled free of the silver fog.

With an expression of relief, and also of sadness, he looked for Walking Buffalo and the horses. They were but specks of movement on the green swath of land at the base of a distant mesa. As he watched, man and horses blended in with the land and could no longer be seen.

With the disappearance of Walking Buffalo, the music weakened swiftly. Even the little that remained was discordant, jarring and unpleasant to the ear. The golden sunlight was rapidly fading.

Anubis jerked as a sudden burst of diabolical laughter of derision burst out behind him. He spun in the direction of the laughter.

In the half light stood Skeleton Man with all his black hairiness and wearing his black finery with top hat. His cave of a mouth was open and he was laughing and slapping his long, skinny leg. He started dancing that jig he had done before and staring at Anubis.

He stopped dancing standing on one leg and ceased laughing. He pointed a bony finger at Anubis and spoke sternly, accusingly. "You're a thief. You've stolen . . ."

Anger seized Anubis and he leapt at Skeleton Man, his arms outstretched to grab his tormentor. They closed on nothing. Skeleton Man had vanished. So too had all the music, all the light. Blackness everywhere.

Anubis awoke lying in the dark vehicle with his head touching the head of Walking Buffalo's corpse. He jerked away, cursing.

Chapter Nine

Dan sat in his favorite place in the Bank Vault Club. He should be studying but could not concentrate on the contents of the thick book opened before him. He had created an enemy, one with much skill at stalking and shooting. Such a man, when he could choose the time and place for his attack, had an excellent chance to succeed in killing his desired victim.

Dan picked up his empty glass and scanned the noisy crowd filling the tables and swinging to the music coming from the band. He was keeping a close watch on a table where five men sat drinking and laughing loudly. He saw Clara near the bar and held up his glass. She nodded her understanding.

Behind the bar, Ray was listening to someone on the phone. He held the phone out toward Dan and silently mouthing, "It's for you".

Dan crossed to the bar and took the phone. He covered one ear with his hand so as to hear above the loud noise in the club.

"Hello."

"What kinds of dreams do you dream, Dan?" came a man's voice.

Dan was silent for a hand full of seconds. He had never expected to hear the voice of his enemy. Instead, the first thing he anticipated was an attack out of the darkness and an exchange of pistol shots. Dan would talk with the man and maybe find out something that could be used to protect the colonel and himself.

"So it's the man with the pistol. Why'd you try to shoot me?"

"You shouldn't have been at the colonel's home," Anubis replied. "Why were you there?"

"A person has to be someplace all the time. And why not by the lake? It's a free world."

"A free world holds much danger."

"That's true." Dan did not like being threatened. "And for everybody."

"I won't miss the next time."

"Come at me anytime you're ready. But tell me your name so I'll know who I'll be fighting."

Dan waited for a response. The phone remained silent, still Dan knew he was connected with the man.

The voice came again, "You can call me Anubis. That's what all my new friends know me by. What's the name of that book you're studying?"

"Ethics in Medicine," he said tersely, and flung a fast look over the patrons in the Club, crowded as usual, and trying to spot the caller. He saw several big men, none of them was talking on a phone.

"Ethics," came the voice. "There are no such thing as ethics. And there's no use looking for me for I'm not there now. I just wanted to look you over in the light."

"What in hell do you want?"

"For your enlightenment, there's no such place as hell. But to the point of my call. I really want to know why you were spying on Colonel Granville?"

"That's my business."

"I know you're studying to be a neuroscientist at the university. So I believe your reason may be to understand Colonel Granville's unique ability to make men dream. Is that the reason?"

"Think whatever you want. And anyway, what's it to you?" Dan hoped the man would say something he could use to protect the colonel and himself.

There was no response from Anubis for a few seconds. Then he spoke in a coaxing tone. "Come tell me, what kind of dreams do you have as an ex-Marine who has seen combat."

Dan remained silent. Let the time build and draw this man Anubis into more conversation.

"Have you been to one of the colonel's dream sessions? What are they like?"

Dan remained silent.

After a moment, Anubis spoke. "The colonel is a very unique person. I sense his destiny and mine are tied together. As for you, Dan, there's nothing you can do to prevent a preordained destiny from happening. In fact, I think you and I shall meet again and take a journey together. And very soon."

The phone clicked off. To Dan the disconnect sound seemed unnaturally loud, had a finality about it. He knew he had been threatened.

As he reached across the bar and hung up the phone, he again checked the crowd in case he had overlooked the man. He saw nobody who could be the person who called himself Anubis.

Dan shoved through the crowd and back to his table. He sat down and looked at the open book. He did not see the pages of text. His mind was swiftly re-running the conversation, searching for something, anything that would help him and the colonel to meet the danger so very imminent. He found nothing and took out his cell phone and dialed.

The colonel answered. "Hello."

"Colonel, this is Dan."

"Hello, Dan. You have news?"

"Yes sir. Your man just called me. I asked his name and he said to call him Anubis. Maybe you can get something out of that."

"I'll think on it. What else?"

"He wanted to know why I was spying on you. That's what he said, spying. I told him it was none of his business. He didn't like that answer. Then he asked me what kind of dreams I had. I didn't answer that one. He said yours and his destinies were tied together. I think he plans to pay both of us a visit that we won't appreciate."

"Be very careful, Dan. I've put you in a dangerous situation. I'd understand if you want out."

"No, sir. I'm in all the way."

"Very well then. I have set up the account for your services. You can withdraw money as you need it. The law firm is named Bannon, Howland & Cleever."

"Thanks, colonel. I'll do the best that I can to identify the stalker quickly so that we can stay ahead of him. But you be ready for him in case he comes at you before that."

"I will. There's something else I've been thinking about. Should I be killed, I want you to continue on with my treatment for the veterans."

Dan was much surprised by the request. "Colonel, I don't have any of your skills. There's no way I can help them."

"Don't downplay what you can do. I believe you have skills you don't yet realize. Once you get your doctorate, then evaluate what you can do."

"That's a fair request and I'll do that."

"Good. This fellow Anubis would be a good specimen for your study in neuroscience."

"I've thought the same thing. But right now I'd rather we found out who he is so we can stop to him."

"I want to know everything that happens so call me anytime. Again I tell you, be on guard at all times."

"I'll do that. Goodbye, colonel."

"Goodbye, Dan."

*****

"I'm glad to get this," Detective Alan Hickman told Dan. Hickman was behind his desk in the police station and looking at Ethan and Dan seated on chairs close by. He held the envelope containing the note Anubis had left for Dan. Hickman was a man of medium height and thin. He appeared tired, harried. "I'll have it checked for fingerprints right away."

Hickman swept his hand over several photos lying on his desk and showing Admiral Essex's bedroom and his dead body lying on the bed. "Perhaps your stalker has some connection with this. This man was killed three nights ago and we have no leads, just a broken window."

Hickman focused on Dan. "Ethan told me his version of the situation. Now tell me yours. Right from the beginning. Don't leave anything out."

Dan looked at Ethan. "Everything?"

"The colonel said to tell everything just like it happened from the dream session to you getting the note and then the phone call."

Dan turned to the detective. "The day after the dream session, the colonel and Ethan came to the Bank Vault Club where I work. The colonel hired me to find this man who he believes is stalking him. And who we now know really is."

"Why you? Do you have some special skill?"

"Not really. He said it was because of my studies in neuroscience at the University. And probably my work with dreams, though he never said that. And maybe because I fight in some bare knuckle fights around town."

Hickman nodded. "All right. Go on."

"So last night I go and act like I'm spying on the colonel at his house on the lake. I find an old Vietnam War Vet living in the bushes near the house. He told me he had seen a man watching the house. Big sonofabitch, the old man told me. Bigger than me. That'd make him over six feet tall."

"This old vet, what was he doing there?"

"Sleeping in a patch of shrubbery near the yard. Had a tent hidden there and stole a little electricity for his heater. I hope you don't bother him for I've hired him to keep an eye on the house and tell me what the stalker does when he comes again. And I believe he will." Dan fell quiet and waited for Hickman to say something.

The detective examined Dan with shrewd policeman's eyes. Then he nodded at the envelope. "Tell me about the note."

"When I get back to my car that I had parked not far from the colonel's house, somebody took a shot at me. They missed as you can see. That note was under my windshield wiper blade. I kept it to check for fingerprints." Dan didn't see any reason to tell Hickman about shooting back.

"The phone call?"

"Last night I got a call at the club from the man who wrote the note. Admitted he had. He asked me what kind of dreams I had. And wanted to know if I had been to one of the colonel's dream sessions. I didn't answer either question. There's a little more about this fellow that's interesting. He asked me the name of the book I was studying. Which means he had been at the club earlier and watching me and wanted me to know it. Said I was an interesting fellow and that he would come visit me. I took that as a threat."

"Threat, eh? I don't suppose he gave his name?"

"Matter of fact, he did. Said to call him Anubis."

"Anubis?"

"That's the name of an ancient Egyptian god."

"Did he say anything that struck you as being strange?"

"Yeah. How he kept talking about dreams. Once in the note. And then several times on the phone call. Seemed to have a fixation on them."

Hickman sat for a time, tapping his fingers on his desk and studying Dan. "All right. I'll have this checked for fingerprints. And for anything else it might tell us. Call me if you discover something new about your stalker."

Chapter Ten

Dan left the Science Building of the University of Chicago and hurried down the steps and off along the walk across the campus. As he approached the main gate, he saw Kristin standing and watching him. He gave her a wave and she returned it with a broad smile.

"Dan, why are we hurrying?" Kristin asked when Dan took her by the arm and guided her toward the street.

"Detective Hickman called me here at the University and asked me to come with him to a murder scene. He said that, since I'm studying the human brain and its ability to reason, he wanted my opinion on something."

"Like what?"

"He didn't say."

Kristin took Dan's hand and squeezed it tightly. "You make me feel good," she said and pressed her shoulders to his to add importance to her words.

"Not as good as you make me feel. In all ways."

"Something that helps both man and woman, can't be bad."

Dan chuckled. "I'll buy that all the way."

* * * * *

As Dan and Kristin came out onto the sidewalk, Dan nodded at a car parked in a no parking zone. "There's Hickman waiting,"

He dug into a pocket and handed Kristin a ring with three keys. "Here, you take the SS. I'm sure Hickman will drive me home after we're done with whatever he's got planned."

"Okay. I'll stop and pick up some things and cook us a good dinner."

"Sounds just right to me."

Kristin stepped close to Dan and gave him a quick kiss on the lips. She spun about and hastened away with a light, happy step toward the parking lot.

Dan climbed into the police car and nodded to Hickman. "Hello."

"Hello, Dan. Good looking girl."

"She sure is. What's up?"

"There's something strange I'm hoping you can help me with," Hickman replied as he drove into the flow of traffic.

"You're not going to tell me now?"

"No. I want you to see it without any comments from me."

"However there is something you can look at while we're driving to the place." Hickman took up a half dozen photos from the seat and handed them to Dan.

"Take a look at these photos and tell me what you see. That fellow isn't sleeping. He's dead, murdered."

Dan scrutinized the first photo of Admiral Essex lying on his bed. Then moved on to the next one taken from a different angle of the same scene, and on to the next one until he had seen them all.

"You see anything odd?"

"This fellow looks like he might have been thinking of something pleasant as he died. Which doesn't make much sense."

"How do you know he died thinking something pleasant?"

"In our studies of sleep and dreaming, we've awakened people up with that same expression on their mugs. They tell us what they were dreaming at the time. It's always something they were finding pleasing."

"What else do you see?"

"Someone was lying beside him when he died, or just before, or just after. You can see the impression of a head on the pillow right near the dead man's. Really close. Like maybe a woman was there."

"Very good."

"What killed him?"

"Do you know Marcaine, Zemuron and curare?"

"I've run into the names in my studies. Both curare and Zemuron are muscle relaxants and make a person unable to move. Both are a poison in large doses. Marcaine is an anesthetic that deadens pain."

"A heavy dose of a mixture of those killed that man. By the way, he was a retired navy admiral."

"And so the questions are, why did someone want him dead?" Dan said. "Why use something so complicated? And why lie near the body? Alive or dead?"

Hickman nodded. "Right. We found dirt on the covers near the foot of the bed so the killer had his shoes on, and most probably the rest of his clothing. The admiral had his pajamas on so it seems no sex was involved. Still the killer got something from killing the men. But what? What's his motive for his killings?"

"Have there been other murderers of this same kind?"

"Several with exactly the same M.O. And we're finding them happening more frequently. Can you think of anything a weirdo might get from killing like this?"

"Not off hand. But you're correct. He must be getting some kind of pleasure from it. Did you find any fingerprints on the note the killer left on my car?"

"None except yours. But we did discover that it's a special kind of paper with unique dimensions. The watermark and the size identified it as being used by just one place. The Chicago Board of Trade. So our man could be a trader of commodities. Or has some way to get hold of that special paper. Maybe we'll find out more from the lab people for they've discovered some very slight impressions of writing on it. They're using special dyes trying to bring it out so it can be read. Something about writing crushing the fibers of the paper and that makes them pick up dye in different amounts. Maybe this is the break I've been waiting for to solve this thing."

"There must be a lot of traders at the Exchange."

"Yeah. Several hundred. I've got men checking every trader that's over six feet tall. I've told my men to start with the tallest and work down."

"To speed it up even more, I suggest that you start with unmarried men."

Hickman gave Dan a knowing look. "I hadn't thought of that. But you're right, single men are the ones most apt to do odd things."

Hickman dialed as he drove. Then spoke into the phone. "Ben, after you sort out the tallest traders, then use being single as the next strongest factor and start your investigation with them."

Hickman paused, listening. "That's what I said. Single. You know. Unmarried. And call me the minute you have a lead."

Hickman closed his phone and pocketed it. He spoke to Dan. "Do you really believe Colonel Granville can see auras?"

"Yes. He'd not lie about that. And he's not alone in making that claim."

"Tell me what you know about them."

"People describe them as halos of light surrounding the human body, and other living things too. They're said to have different colors depending upon the condition of the physical body. Photos have been published that show these auras. They're called Kirlian photos. I've seen some of them and they look real. I've even seen some photos of plants that seem to show the images of recently severed parts. As if the parts were still attached to the body of the plant."

Hickman shook his head. "The whole idea seems damn strange to me."

"Maybe not strange. Every cell of the body is a little electrical dynamo, and those little dynamos are what keeps us alive. So if every cell is producing electricity, why wouldn't our bodies give off an electrical discharge that would show as an aura if the frequency could be seen? A halo of some sort?"

"Halo? You mean like what Christ was suppose to have had?" Hickman chuckled.

"Maybe something like that."

"Here we are," said Hickman.

He slowed and pulled into the entrance of St. Cashimir Catholic Cemetery and onward up a winding paved road to the rear portion. He stopped near a police car where two uniformed policemen were standing with a man in work clothes. Off a few steps, a body was visible lying among the tombstones.

"The dead man is an Indian," Hickman said to Dan. "Or so the officer who called it in said. And that he was laid out like in an undertaker parlor. Some of the other men were killed with that concoction of chemicals and were laid out in that same manner. That's why I wanted you to come along to maybe help me figure out what it all means."

"I'm certainly no expert, but I'll do what I can," Dan replied. He got out of the car and followed Hickman to the group of men.

Hickman spoke to the nearest cop. "Any one tramp the scene? Disturb anything?"

The cop pointed at the man in work clothes. "Just the caretaker who found him. Said he didn't touch anything. And I took a quick look. Then I called homicide."

Hickman nodded. He spoke to Dan. "Let's have a look."

Hickman and Dan walked among the tombstones to where Walking Buffalo lay stretched out on his back on the ground. His clothes were neatly arranged and his arms were crossed over his chest. He had a pleased, even a happy expression on his face. A half dollar held each eye lid closed. He could just be sleeping.

"He has on welders clothing, you can see the burn marks on them from hot metal, and on his shoes too," Hickman said. "I'm guessing that he's one of the Zuni's working on the high rises being built around town. I don't see any obvious wounds on him. Let's look for puncture marks."

He knelt beside the body. "Ah, here is one on his lower arm."

He took a knife from his pocket and working carefully, cut open the legs of Walking Buffalo's pants covering the upper thighs. On the second leg, was the puncture wound from the injection of a needle.

"Just like the others. My man killed this Indian. What's he getting that's worth killing for?"

Hickman looked up at Dan. "This sure doesn't look like a robbery. And it wasn't done by a sadist. It's not a crime of passion. All the bodies are treated gently. You're the brain specialist. Talk to me. Tell me what kind of a man did this."

"First off, the man didn't kill the Indian because he hated him. That shows by the care he took in laying out the body. He even straightened his clothes. So why kill him? The obvious answer is that the Indian had something he wanted. I have no idea what that could've been."

"I've been trying to figure out what it was that drew him to all his victims? We can't find anything that they all have in common. One was a poet, one a state senator, an ex-fighter pilot, an admiral, and now an Indian steel worker."

Dan stared at Walking Buffalo's corpse as he considered Hickman's words. Then an answer came.

"But they do have something in common. Each is different from all the others, that's true. But they are all similar in that they come from a very small, select group of people. How many poets are there in Chicago? How many fighter pilots? Now he's stalking Colonel Granville who is surely unique. Our killer is very discriminating."

"Yes. I see that. Now we need to find out if he was killed here in the cemetery or brought here afterwards. The coroner can tell us that."

"This is an isolated place and a good one for killing, or getting rid of a body," Dan said. "I think the Indian is here probably because of its isolation, but also because being among the dead could be a sign of the respect the killer had for him."

"Do you think dreams and auras enter into the reason for all these killings?"

"I've got this gut feeling that they do. But I sure as hell don't know how."

"Here comes the coroner." Hickman said and glancing at the approaching vehicle. "He'll be able to tell us how long ago this fellow was killed. But before he gets the body, I'm going to give the area around here a good going over. I don't expect to find anything useful for the fellow is damn careful not to leave anything behind. When I'm finished here, I'll take you wherever you want to go."

"I'll get out of your way," Dan said and moved to stand with the police officers as the coroner's vehicle drove up and stopped.

Chapter Eleven

Dan entered the Science Building, climbed to the second floor and continued along the hallway to the area marked Dept. of Brain and Cognitive Science. He entered and moved ahead to a second room marked Sleep Study Lab and went inside.

He stopped behind the four graduate students, two young men and two young women in their late twenties, seated and watching a large flat screen monitor. They were also observing, through a glass wall, a young man lying asleep on his back on a cot with a thin sheet covering him. Scores of small metal terminals were attached to his shaved skull, with a cord extending from each. The cords came together into a thick electrical cable that led through the soundproof glass wall to the monitor of the graduate students.

Dan focused on the monitor where a transparent skull with a semitransparent brain inside was rotating slowly. Various regions of the brain flashed bright electrical discharges in synchrony with the location of the firing synapses of the sleeper's brain.

"It seems that I've arrived a little late," Dan said.

The four quickly turned to Dan and gave him friendly looks.

Paul spoke. "Well, look at who finally showed up at the lab."

"I hope I haven't missed anything important," Dan said.

"Not yet," replied James. "Tom has been asleep about an hour. He's due his first erection any time now."

"How many terminals are attached to his skull?"

"Ninety three," James answered.

"That number should give a good read," Dan said. "How'd you get him to shave his head and be the study subject?"

James smiled broadly and nodded at Tamara and Casey. "He agreed to it after Casey and Tamara both promised they'd use their lovely female bodies to help him get it down."

Both women show sudden embarrassment. Tamara called out quickly. "James, you're a lying ass."

"You damn well know we never promised such a thing," Casey added hurriedly.

James laughed hugely. "Yes, you both did. And I'll prove it when Tom wakes up."

Tamara spoke pleadingly to Paul, the second man. "Tell Dan that James is a big liar."

"Dan already knows James is a joker," Paul said.

Both girls turned to Dan. There was a sparkle of humor in their eyes for their anger was mostly put on.

"Dan, I've had enough of James. He deserves a good pounding. Slug him hard for me."

Dan just smiled for he knew it was mostly a game with the four.

Paul spoke hurriedly. "Look at Tom. We're getting action."

The five concentrated on the sheet over Tom's crotch that was rising as his prick stiffened and rose. They turned away from Tom to look at the monitor.

"Here's the signals of Tom's first erection," James said.

"One hour and thirty six minutes," Paul added. "Pretty much on schedule for the first of the three or so erections a man has during a night's sleep."

James spoke. "Wow. Look at that. Just about every synapsis in Tom's brain is firing. The only time we know for certain what a man's mind is concentrating on is when he gets a hard-on."

James turned to the girls. "I wonder which one of you two lovely ladies he's having sex with." He grinned wolfishly. "Now stop dreaming about what he's doing. Remember you're scientists."

"Oh, shut up," Tamara said, getting miffed at James.

"I'd like to be able to see what he sees," Dan said.

Casey nodded and said, "If we had more sensitive equipment, maybe we could turn the electrical pulses from the firing synapses into pictures on the monitor."

"We're years away from having that kind of equipment," Paul said.

"Yes, years," Tamara agreed. "We need something many times more sensitive than this scanner. Even a human brain can't read another person's thoughts. And it's the most sensitive thing we know of."

"Some people's eyes and brain are so sensitive that they can see another person's aura," Dan said.

Tamara looked at Dan. "I've read that. Do you believe it?"

"I know a man who says he can. And I believe him."

Casey spoke, "Really? I'd like to meet him."

"All right. I'll take you to see him the next time he has one of his dream sessions for the vets."

"How about taking all of us?" Paul said.

"All right, all of you. It's a date." Dan studied the faces of the four. They joked and kidded around, still they were an intelligent lot and no better group could he pose the question that had been on his mind these past two days. "Now consider this and give me your thoughts. If one man can see a human aura, why can't there be another man out of the billions of humans on the planet who can do more than that. One who can actually tune into the electrical signals of firing synapses of another person and see what that person sees? Create the same picture? Or something close?"

The four listeners focused intently on Dan.

"Everybody's brain is constructed the same way," Tamara said. "Yet there are many levels of intelligence. So, if there's different levels of intelligence why can't there be different levels of sensitivity to other people's thoughts."

"Theoretically it's possible," Paul added. "But how about the receiving brain? How could its thoughts, which are always turned on, be halted so it could receive the transmitted signals?"

"That would be a roadblock, and a big one," Dan acknowledged, knowing it could well be the factor that prevented what he was suggesting.

Casey spoke. "I don't think a brain could somehow be controlled to that extent. It would have to be literally shut down to allow the electrical signals from another brain to enter and create a similar picture. We're talking about one brain allowing another to dominate it."

"Unless the receiving brain was defective in some way," Paul said.

"Maybe not defective," Casey said. "One wired in a different way from ours. In a way that allowed the person who possessed it to reach out and capture another person's thoughts. It could be a brain superior to ours."

"How about in sleep?" Dan asked. "Suppose one person was asleep? Or both were?"

James shook his head. "Even in sleep, the human brain is busy with its own thoughts, its own dream pictures."

"Suppose both brains were dreaming," Dan said as he recalled his dream session with the colonel, and the beautiful red headed girl that cried. "Could there then be a melding of two people's dreams with each adding something to the dream?"

Dan checked the faces of the four, seeing the intense expression as each pursued the question in his or her own special way.

"Let's take it one step further," Dan said. "Suppose two people were within each others' aura and one man couldn't dream. Would it then be possible for the dream of one man to be seen by the second? For both to see the same images and to feel the same emotions?"

"I'd say it's possible," Paul said. "And there are those rare individuals who can't dream."

Dan rubbed his chin as new thoughts about old events came to him. His eyes lit up as a possibility crystallized into near certainty. "Such a person, such a human, might feel something was missing in him. Might even know what that something was."

Dan laughed lightly and included the group of four with a sweep of his eyes. "A man once asked me what kind of dreams I dreamed. His voice had a kind of sadness. I didn't recognize it at the time, but it was the same tone a person uses who desires the thing the other person has, but that he doesn't. Do you suppose . . ."

Dan fell silent as he considered the ramifications of what he now believed might well be true.

James was looking at the monitor. He called out. "Damnation. I feel sorry for you two gals. Look at Tom's signals. He's dreaming about something besides sex with one of you. He won't be needing your beautiful bodies."

All five focus on the monitor.

"Damn, that's too bad," Tamara said with a mock sigh.

All laughed, then quieted as Dan's cell phone rang. He pulled it from his pocket and walked to the rear of the room.

"Dan here," he said.

"This is Hickman. We've deciphered the writing on that note of yours. It's an order to buy a number of wheat contracts. Our man could be a wheat trader at the Mercantile Exchange."

"That's damn good news."

"It sure is," Hickman said. "By trying to be smart with you, he may have given himself away. I'm going to the Exchange to examine the files of the traders in the wheat pit. The manager has agreed to keep his office open after the exchange closes so that the traders won't see what I'm doing. You want to join me there in say two hours?"

"Yeah. I'd like to see the files too. I want to catch that SOB."

"Good. See you there."

Dan called to the four graduate students. "I'm going to have to leave you. There's a place I have to be in a little while. And before that, I want to review that research paper Doctor Will Crandall wrote last year on his dreams studies at Yale."

* * * * *

Dan was in his cubbyhole office at the University and deep into the report of Crandall's study on dreams when Kristin arrived and entered. She wore a gray coat and a perky, gray hat cocked over an eye. She smiled brightly at Dan.

"Are you ready to leave?" Kristin asked.

"Something has come up. Hickman wants me to come down to the Mercantile Exchange and help him cull through the wheat traders and maybe pick out our killer."

"He's found something that leads him there?" Kristin asked.

"Yes, that note I gave him."

"That's too bad. I thought we'd go to your place and have some good loving."

"That was my plan too. But I promised to help him. Why don't you drive me down to the Exchange and then take the car and do what you have to do. Then meet me at my apartment later this evening."

"I hate to wait. But I'll tough it out. I could say that the loving will be better from having to wait. But I don't think it will be,"

"Just hang in there," Dan said. He grabbed Kristin and gave her a huge hug.

* * * * *

Kristin drove the SS up to the curb in front of the Chicago Mercantile Exchange and stopped. It was past closing time for the Exchange and the street held few people.

Inside the SS, Dan leaned and gave Kristin a kiss on the lips. She pressed her lips to his, holding the kiss for a few seconds before pulling away.

"I'll see you whenever we're finished here, probably take a couple of hours," Dan said.

"I'll have some chow ready for us to build our strength for afterwards."

"Right." Dan touched Kristin's cheek. "Damn, it's tough to wait." He climbed out and hurried across the sidewalk toward the Exchange.

Kristin shifted the SS into gear and drove away.

Dan pushed open the double doors of the Exchange and approached the guard's desk located so that the guard could inspect all who entered. The guard watched him with questioning eyes.

"My name is Dan Gallatin. Detective Hickman said I should meet him here."

"He told me you'd be coming. Go straight back and up the stairs to the second floor. He's in Miller's office, third door on the right." The guard chucked a thumb over his shoulder.

"Right."

Dan hastened across the lobby and up the stairs to Miller's office. Hickman and a second man were at a large table covered with personnel files. Both men looked up as Dan entered.

Hickman lifted a hand in greeting to Dan. He spoke to Miller, "This is Dan Gallatin. He's from the university. I'd like for him to review the files of the traders with me."

"Glad to meet you, Gallatin," said Miller, a short man, mostly bald, with penetrating eyes. "Have a seat. I'll leave you two to your work. The files are arranged in alphabetical order. Don't take anything out of them. If you need a copy of something, tell me and I'll make it for you. I'll be in my office next door."

Miller left the room, leaving the door open to his office.

Hickman shoved part of the personnel files in front of Dan. "Have at them," he said.

Dan eyed the pile, then looked at Hickman. "Before we start that, I have a theory about our man. Why he lies down beside the people he kills."

"All right? Let's have it."

"It's going to be hard to believe."

"Well, hell, Dan. Why don't you just tell me and let me be the judge of what I believe. I've had some damn weird cases."

"It's a mind game."

"All murders are mind games. At least in the mind of the killer."

"That's right. But this one isn't about rage, or revenge. or one of the usual reasons to kill."

"What then? Let's have it." Hickman began to tap the table with his fingers, growing tired of the buildup.

"I believe our man is something damn different from what we've ever seen before. I think that he might be able to hitch onto the dreams of sleeping people. And I mean that literally. He lies down beside a sleeper and by some quirk in his brain, can hitch onto their dreams."

"And why would he want to do that?" Hickman asked doubtfully. "Even if he could."

"Yes, why? To my way of reasoning, the only reason would be if he couldn't dream on his own."

Hickman shook his head. "All people can dream."

"No. That's not so. There are those few individuals who can't dream."

"I didn't know that. But why does he kill them? Why not just dream along with them and then get up and leave when it's over."

"Yes, why not? Some of the sleepers might wake up and he kills them so as to keep out of trouble. But not all would."

Hickman laughed. "Maybe he goes to heaven with them. It's been reported many times that people who have near death experiences have a wonderful, joyful experience."

Dan, being very serious, said, "That'd be a good reason, all right. If two people could share the same dream while sleeping, then why couldn't they share the same dream, the same scene and other dimensions of that world the dying man was experiencing? Though I wouldn't call it dreaming at that stage for there's no waking up."

"I was joking," Hickman said. Seeing Dan's seriousness, Hickman made a faint smile.

"Maybe you were. But I've come to believe that there are dimensions beyond those we know about. And what we've just said fits everything we know."

"Except that thing about hitching onto someone else's dream. We don't know if that is possible. Do you realize how crazy that all sounds?"

"Real crazy."

"Anything else to add to that wild idea?"

"Just this. That's why he chooses the people he does to dream with, the ones that could provide him with unique and exciting dreams. And that's why he's stalking the colonel. He surely is a rare person and would have rare dreams."

"That all fits what we've observed. But it's God awful far out. Give me time to get my head around it all. For now, let's see who among these thirty two wheat traders that are over six feet tall might be my man. And your Anubis."

"First, I'd like to try something if Miller will work with us. Just maybe there's a quicker way to get at the man's identity. If he's here in this pile of personnel files."

Dan went to the door of Miller's office and called inside. "Mr. Miller, can we have a minute of your time?"

"Sure," Miller said and came into the room with Dan and Hickman. "What can I do for you?"

"Do you know all the men working in the wheat pit?"

"I'm down in the pit part of every day. So I know them all by name. As to their personal side, some more than others."

"Do any men ever talk about their dreams?"

"I heard some say they've dreamed the market will go up, or it'll go down."

"Have you heard one particular man ask other men what their dreams are about?"

Miller pondered that a moment. "Yes. There is one man who I've heard ask about other people's dreams."

Hickman leaned forward with interest. "What's his name? You do have a name?"

"Sure. His name is Krafton. Marcus Krafton."

"What size man is he?"

"Big man. Strongly built. Moves quick even if he is big."

Dan and Hickman gave each other knowing looks. Hickman nodded.

"How long has he been working here?"

"A little over a year."

Hickman quickly began to sort through the files. Pulled one out and opened it.

"You're right. Started here in July of last year. Before that, he was a trader at the San Francisco Stock Exchange."

"What's this all about?" Miller asked

"You may have helped us solve a crime. I can't say more than that. Will you leave us alone? And don't say a word to anybody about this."

"All right, I won't," Miller said and left the room.

"I know a cop in Frisco I want to talk with," Hickman said quickly. He took out his cell phone, checked his listing of phone numbers and dialed.

He spoke into the phone. "Sorenson, hello. This is Hickman in Chicago. How're things out your way?"

Hickman listened. Then said, "Same here, a whole lot on my plate. I have something new here and I want to talk with you about it. Do you have any unsolved murders where the victim was laid out all neat and careful like. Maybe the killer even laid down beside his victim."

Hickman listened again. "Exactly so. When was your last one?"

Hickman's expression became grim. "Well, my friend, I may have identified your man here in Chicago. I've got to go now but I'll keep you informed."

He snapped his phone closed and aimed hard eyes at Dan. "The very same MO. I'll put a team together and go pick up Krafton. You got a ride home?"

"Don't worry about me. You go get Krafton. I'll catch a cab."

"Right. The quicker the better. I don't want another corpse."

Hickman hastily jotted down an address from the file, turned to Miller's office and called out in a loud voice. "Miller, we're done for now. Thanks."

"Let's move fast," Hickman said to Dan.

Chapter Twelve

Anubis sat in his Porsche parked on the dark night street half a block from Dan's apartment. The apartment house and the unlit parking lot behind it were within his view. He had made himself comfortable, at least as much as was possible for a big man in the seat of a Porsche. He had been there for nearly an hour, and he meant to wait for the man to come no matter how long that might be. Now he watched the cars passing on the street, and the few people that walked by on the sidewalk dimly illuminated by a distant streetlight.

He came to quick attention as Dan's SS rolled along the street and turned into the alley that led to the parking lot. He climbed out of the Porsche and hastened to overtake the SS, catching it just as it drove into the parking lot. The SS came to a stop with Anubis close behind it. The headlights went off.

Anubis pulled a pistol from his coat pocket, stepped around the SS and jerked open the driver's door. He pointed the pistol inside.

With the opening of the door, the inside dome light flashed on. Kristin, behind the steering wheel, looked up startled. Seeing Anubis with the pistol pointing into her face, she grabbed the door handle and yanked hard to shut the door.

Anubis stopped the closing of the door with a hand. "Goddamn," he muttered with surprise and staring down at Kristin.

"Who the hell are you?" he growled angrily.

Frightened, Kristin considered screaming and hoped somebody would hear her and come to her aid. The pistol and the size of the man kept her quiet.

Anubis slapped her a stinging blow across the face. "Who are you?"

The slap brought anger to join Kristin's fear. She was in danger, and as in combat, she must fight her way to safety.

Anubis quickly checked the street. Nobody was paying attention to what was happening in the dark parking lot. He caught hold of Kristin's coat front and jerked her out of the car. As she came to her feet, she struck at him with her fists, aiming to land a blow under the chin and into the man's neck, a vulnerable place even for a big man. Her strike missed and she half broke her hand against the man's thick boned jaw.

Anubis rotated Kristin half a turn and clamped a hand over her mouth. He encircled her waist and trapped one arm and lifted her off her feet. He was surprised the woman had not screamed, instead she had struck him a strong blow.

Kristin reached up and backward with her free hand and stabbed with stiffened fingers for the man's eyes. She missed the eyes and felt the flesh of his cheek rip.

"Damn you." Anubis growled. He slammed Kristin's head against the side of the car.

As Kristin went limp, he grabbed her up in his arms and hurried to the Porsche. He stuffed her into the passenger seat and buckled her in tightly with the safety harness. He hastened to the driver's seat and sent the Porsche speeding away.

Kristin moaned. She became conscious with a throbbing pain bursting alive in her head. She hurriedly looked around and saw Anubis. Her fear surged and she fought to control it. She had been in many dangerous places before and had escaped alive. However, then she had a gun and was equal to any man. Now she was up against a man with strength much greater than hers. Even so, there had to be a way to escape. Who was he? He had looked surprised at finding her in the car. Which meant he had been expecting to see Dan in the SS. Could this be the killer that Dan was hunting?

"Let me out," Kristin said, her voice in a conversational tone. "Please, just let me go. I won't say anything. I promise I won't."

"I know you won't for you're going with me. And if you scream or try to jump out of the car, I'll break your neck."

Anubis was silent for a moment. Then he spoke, "I'd planned to share this evening's entertainment with Dan. But you've prevented that. So I'm going to see the colonel. He should be even better entertainment than Dan."

Anubis looked away from the street to Kristin. "I've never dreamed with a woman. However, I like the way you fight and I may make an exception with you. After all, life is about experimenting with new things. What kind of dreams do you have?"

Kristin saw a possible escape route. "You wouldn't like my dreams. Unless you're gay. You gay?"

Anubis laughed. "That won't work. Now just sit there quietly and be a good little girl and plan how you'll escape when I let my guard down."

Minutes later, Anubis pulled off the road and stopped the Porsche near the lane leading to the colonel's home on the lake. The moment the car stopped, Kristin stabbed the release on the seatbelt and it snapped free. She pulled at the door release.

Anubis caught Kristin and struck her a blow to the side of the head. Half unconscious, she slumped in the seat.

Anubis took a syringe from the cubby hole. "I'm going to give you a little shot of something to be certain you'll remain here until I decide whether or not I want to dream with you. You have spirit, so I'm interested in discovering what kind of afterlife you would create for yourself? Now don't move, this'll only sting."

Kristin stared at the syringe. Then up at Anubis, who gingerly touched the bruises on her face. Kristin flinched. Then held still under the man's fingers. Hating him. Fearing him.

Anubis moved the syringe to Kristin's thigh and injected a portion of its contents. Her muscles relaxed, her eyes closed, her breathing slowed to a portion of normal.

* * * * *

Dan got out of the cab in front of his apartment house and paid the cabbie. He was looking forward to a warm greeting from Kristin. He unlocked the door and stepped inside. The apartment was dark.

"Kristin, you asleep?" Dan called out. "Kristin, wake up and feed this hungry fellow."

Only silence greeted Dan's call and a chill washed over him. He hurried to the bedroom, flung open the door and flipped on the light. The room was empty.

He hurried to the window and looked out onto the parking lot. The SS was parked in its usual place.

Dan rushed from the apartment house to the SS. The keys were dangling from the ignition. A bag of groceries was on the rear seat. Fear for Kristin surged through him. Goddamn you Anubis. Or are you Marcus Krafton? Dan had to know the answer to that. He hastily dug his cell phone from a pocket and dialed.

He spoke when the phone was answered. "Hickman, this is Gallatin. Did you find Krafton?"

"He's not here. We went inside and whoever lives here is away."

"Somebody's got my friend Kristin. It has to be Anubis."

"Do you know where he might take her?"

"No. He could take her anyplace. She was in my SS. Anubis could've thought it was me driving it and found Kristin instead. I've got to gamble that he's going to the colonel's house on the lake."

"Why would you think that place?"

"I'm desperate. Since he was looking for me and didn't find me, he may go for the colonel. What are you going to do now that Krafton isn't home?"

"Stake out the place and take him when he shows up," Hickman replied.

"Call me if you see him."

"I will."

Dan pocketed the phone and scooted in under the wheel of the SS, keyed the ignition and peeled rubber out of the parking lot and half way down the block. He rocketed ahead dodging traffic like a man gone mad.

Two cops in a police cruiser going in the opposite direction saw the SS flash past. They make a U-turn in traffic and gave chase with sirens wailing.

Dan tromped the gas pedal to the metal. The SS was made for quick turns and reversal of directions and Dan used all of its fine characteristics. He sped down alleys, turned and slid into a reverse direction and hurtled back past the police cruiser. Then another alley, and another, and wheeled back into his original direction. There was no sign of the police cruiser. Lost behind in an alley. He gave the powerful engine gas and hurried onward.

Dan cruised along the road to the colonel's house with just parking lights on. He saw the Porsche by the side of the road. His pulse sped, that had to belong to Anubis. He stopped and climbed out of the SS. With pistol drawn, he stole upon the Porsche.

Warily, Dan peered in through a window, and saw the night shrouded form of Kristin slumped down in the passenger seat of the car. He quickly opened the door and felt Kristin's neck for a pulse, found it and checked her breathing. She was alive and he shivered with relief.

"Kristin, wake up," Dan said and shaking her. "We've got to get out of here."

Kristin showed no response. Dan shook her roughly and still got no response. She had been either drugged or knocked unconscious, and he had no time to determine which one it was. He unbuckled the belt and pulled her out of the Porsche and into his arms. He hastened into the nearby woods and laid her down gently on the leaf covered ground.

"I'll be back, Kristin," Dan whispered.

He ran back to the road and onward to the tree lined driveway to the colonel's house, and up it to the edge of the patch of shrubbery where he had met Frank Tanner. The colonel's home was dark and silent.

Dan turned to the shrubbery. "Frank, you in there?"

There was no reply. Dan did not want to speak more loudly, so he moved closer to the shrubbery. He tripped on something heavy in the dark and looked down.

Frank lay on the ground. Dan hastily checked for a pulse in Frank's neck. He found none.

Dan sprinted toward the house, then slowed as he drew close, and crept onward watching keenly ahead. A rear door stood open, and he soundlessly entered a storage room containing shelving full of various items. He crossed the room to a doorway faintly outlined by some kind of a light. He cautiously peered into the room and saw the light came from a computer screen.

Dan heard raspy breathing and stepped silently into the room. The sergeant of Marines lay on the floor just inside the doorway. His head was twisted at an unnatural angle. The sound came from the sergeant. Dan looked further into the room. Near the far wall, Colonel Granville lay on the floor. Lying beside him was a big man with his head touching that of the colonel. A syringe was in the man's hand.

* * * * *

Colonel Granville, in full uniform with all his many medals, was at the controls of a space ship hurtling through space toward a magnificent galaxy with huge whirling arms of brilliantly colored suns. The celestial orchestra was playing the grand music of the universe. A broad smile wreathed the colonel's face, a face that was no longer scarred. His body was healed and in the best of health. A truly handsome fellow. He was making the great space journey to the stars that he had always wanted, dreamed about, a journey that had no returning.

Anubis stood two steps behind the colonel and looked in the same direction. He was smiling with the pure joy of the flight through space. The music of the celestial orchestra flooded his body and made every cell, every nerve ending strum with rapture. He concentrated his mind on the music, absorbing it, storing it so that he would be able to recall it again and again when he desired to listen to its pure, grand tones.

* * * * *

Dan leapt across the room and upon Anubis and dragged him away from the colonel. He fell upon the man and began pounding him with both fists.

Anubis jerked back to the here and now of the colonel's bedroom. His eyes opened and his powerful arms came up to protect himself from Dan's fists. He lashed out and landed a solid blow to Dan's face, knocking him off and sending him reeling backward.

Anubis surged up from the floor and sprang at Dan. They struck each other with powerful blows, hammering each other with both fists. They reeled about the room, locked in combat, straining against each other, striking savage blows. Furniture was shoved aside, upended. The computer, lamps, and other objects fell and were tramped upon and broken. Each man was intent on mutilating, killing his adversary.

Anubis landed a mighty blow on Dan's chest and drove him backward. Dan tripped over a chair and fell, his head slammed against the wall as he went down. Half stunned, Dan struggled to rise, for to stay down was to die.

Anubis laughed and fell upon Dan and pounded him savagely with a flurry of blows, driving him down on hands and knees on top of the broken glass screen of the computer. Dan felt the glass stabbing into his hands and knees. Anubis was the stronger man and the fight was lost.

Unless. Unless. Dan closed his hand around a long jagged piece of broken glass from the monitor and struck upward. He felt the glass penetrate Anubis' neck, slicing so easily through the flesh, to stop abruptly jammed up against his spine.

A crimson geyser of blood erupted from Anubis' neck and fell upon Dan. He rolled away from the injured man.

Anubis remained perfectly motionless for a second. Then he understood the wound he had received. He shoved a finger into the gash in the carotid artery to stop the fountain of blood. The cut was too large and the blood continued to spray out. He thrusts two fingers into the gash. The flow diminished but little.

Terror flooded Anubis for he knew the wound was fatal. He began to tremble from the large loss of blood. He sank down and sat on the floor.

* * * * *

Anubis stood in a world of dark shadows and total silence. He peered hard into the shadows full of shapes, with all so distorted that none could be identified. He hastily felt his neck. He had no wounds, not even from Dan's fists. Anubis slowly pivoted and stared about.

A figure moved toward him through the gloom. From the figure came the wild laugh of the Skeleton Man.

The figure drew closer and Anubis could make out the Skeleton Man with his black hairiness, and wearing his black finery with top hat. His cave of a mouth was open and he was laughing. He slapped his long, skinny leg and began to dance that jig Anubis had seen before.

He stopped his dance. His laughter ceased and he pointed a bony finger at Krafton.

"You're a thief for you stole my name," Skeleton Man said in a harsh, accusing voice.

He tapped himself on the chest. "I am Anubis and you are in the domain where I rule. You've made a fatal mistake by coming here for I'll not allow you to leave."

Anubis gave Krafton a kingly smile. "I wait through the ages for men like you to come to me. Now I'm going to weigh your heart to see what kind of afterlife you've earned by your deeds."

"You don't exist," Krafton said. "This is all just a dream and I'll prove it."

Krafton leapt at Anubis, his arms outstretched to grab his tormentor. Anubis didn't vanish as before. He was solid as a stone statue and Krafton was stopped, plastered against him.

Anubis took Krafton by the shoulders and lifted him as if he were but a feather. Anubis's face was wreathed with malevolent delight as he stared into Krafton's eyes.

"You love death so much that you have killed many men to journey with them into the afterlife. And since you do enjoy death so much, I shall help you die in the scores of ways humans have devised to kill one another."

Anubis roughly shook Krafton. "Pay attention now for I'm going to tell you a little history about humans. Every religion had its torture devices and their leaders had oceans of blood on their hands. They tortured those people who strayed from what was considered the true religion, and kill that person if he or she would not recant all other beliefs. The Greeks had their Brazen Bull which is one of my favorites. The condemned person was placed inside the metal bull and a fire was built beneath to roast the person. The bull was designed so that the person's screams of pain sounded like the bull bellowing."

Anubis again shook Krafton, even more roughly.

"Listen. Listen to me. The Spanish, oh the Spanish, they were the greatest of all in the many ways they had to torture a man or woman to make him or her recant. To name a few, they had The Inquisitional Chair, The Rack, The Head Crusher, The Saw. Now The Saw was truly that for it was used to saw a person into pieces, from crotch to head."

Anubis stared into Krafton's frightened eyes and continued to speak. "I see that you are tired of my history lesson. So on with the first act of your show, and it is your show. Remember now, there are a thousand acts to this show and you are the star in every one."

Instantly a scene appeared with Krafton bound with rope to a stout wooden post. A large mound of wood was piled around his feet. He began to struggle wildly, using all his great strength trying to break loose as he watched Anubis approach with a torch.

Anubis' face was rigid with determination to inflict horrible pain upon Krafton. He ignited the wood with the torch. Flames sprang up all red and orange. They grew rapidly. Krafton screamed in horrible pain.

Anubis danced his famous jig and laughed with hilarious joy. He danced around and around Krafton as the flames engulfed him.

Instantly, a new scene appeared. Krafton was chained to a medieval rack, his feet to one end and his outstretched arms to the opposite. Anubis was turning the windlass of the rack. He was really leaning into his task, hauling mightily on the spokes of the windlass.

Krafton was stretched to the limit before his tendons broke and his arms were torn from their sockets. He was screaming with unbelievable pain.

Anubis made a powerful twist of the spokes of the windlass.

Instantly, a new scene appeared. Krafton's hands were tied behind his back, his legs were also bound, and he was on his knees. His neck was outstretched and lying across a wooden chopping block.

Anubis was standing and leaning on the handle of a huge ax, an ancient medieval broadax used for decapitation. He was looking down at Krafton with a bemused expression. He started to chuckle. That grew to a laugh. That peaked with a howl of laughter. He controlled himself with an effort and raised the ax high.

He looked down at Krafton and said with a smile, "Get ready now for this may sting a little."

Anubis swung the ax powerfully down. Krafton's head was neatly severed from his body and rolled a few feet away.

Anubis dropped the ax and snatched up Krafton's head. He slapped the face smartly and looked into its eyes.

In that instant just before Krafton's brain died, an expression of total terror flashed across the face.

Seeing the expression, Anubis began to laugh with immense pleasure.

* * * * *

Dan came to his feet and stood weakly in the shambles of the room in Colonel Granville's home. He was bruised and battered and ached in scores of places. He looked down at Krafton's body lying in a pool of blood. The spear of glass had done its deadly work.

He staggered to the colonel and bent over him. The man was dead. His face was wreathed in an expression of immense joy.

"You will be greatly missed, colonel. Especially by the vets like me." Dan closed the lids over the crystal coated orbs. "Have a grand voyage into the next world, colonel," he said.

About The Author

F.M. Parker has worked as a sheepherder, lumberman, sailor, geologist, and as a manager of wild horses, wild, free roaming buffalo and livestock grazing. For several years he was the manager of five million acres of Public Domain Land in eastern Oregon. His highly acclaimed novels include the *Coldiron* Series, *The Searcher*, *The Assassins*, *Predators and Prey*, and *The Shadow Man*.

Coming Soon!

F.M. PARKER'S

THE ASSASSINS
(a.k.a. A Score to Settle)

The time is 1847, and the place is turbulent New Orleans during the staging of American forces, army and navy, for the invasion of Mexico with its lucrative army contracts, and with the plague of yellow fever killing scores of people each week.

Timothy Wollfolk, traveling from Cincinnati to New Orleans, is shot by robbers and thrown into the flooding Mississippi River. Lew Fannin, ex-Texas lawman on his way to join the army and fight in the invasion of Mexico, comes upon the killing and shoots the robbers…

Two violent strands of dramatic conflict are set into motion against the background of troops moving to war in Mexico, and a scourge of yellow fever decimating the city. In this violence, Wollfolk and Fannin must decide if they are enemies of allies. Their decision leads to two violent battles; Morissot against Kelty; Tim and Lew against the members of "The Ring".

**For more information
visit:** www.SpeakingVolumes.us

Now Available!

F.M. PARKER'S
FICTION HISTORICAL NOVELS

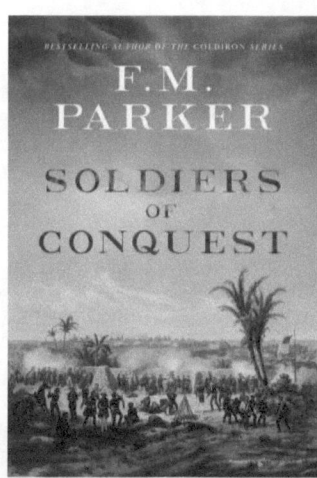
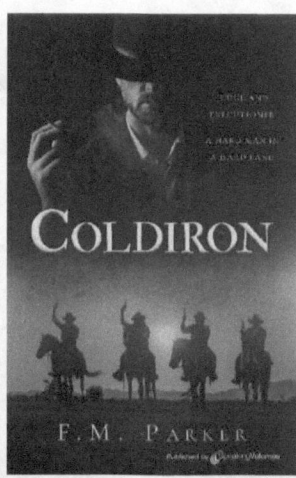

**For more information
visit:** www.SpeakingVolumes.us

Now Available!
SPUR AWARD-WINNING AUTHOR
ROD MILLER

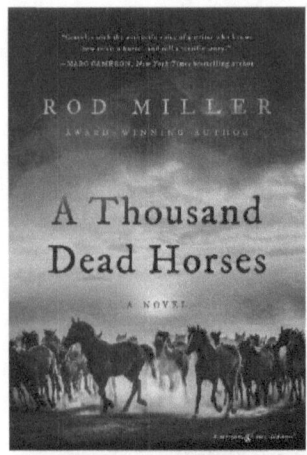  

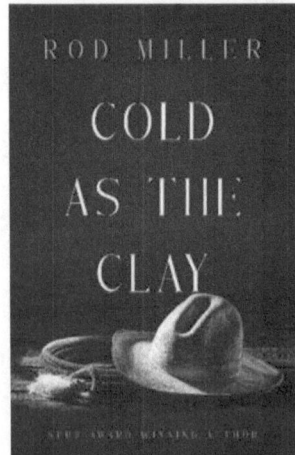  

**For more information
visit:** www.SpeakingVolumes.us

Now Available!
AWARD WINNING AUTHOR
MARK WARREN

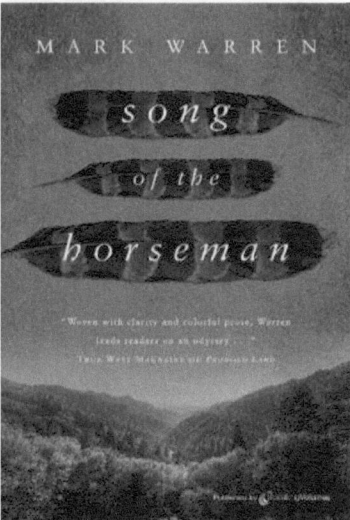

**For more information
visit: www.SpeakingVolumes.us**

Now Available!

BRIEN A. ROCHE

THE PROHIBITION SERIES
BOOK 1 – BOOK 2 – BOOK 3

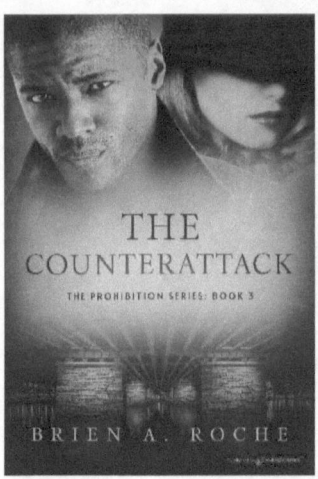

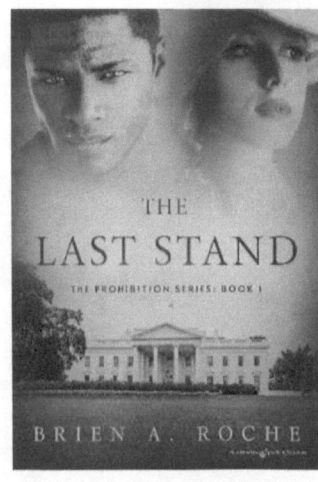

**For more information
visit: www.SpeakingVolumes.us**

www.ingramcontent.com/pod-product-compliance
Lightning Source LLC
LaVergne TN
LVHW041708060526
838201LV00043B/636